Caïssa

The chessboard rushed in from nowhere and the darkness of the black zone fell away. Her red pieces surrounded her, knights and rooks and bishops and pawns. There were no white pieces.

She advanced a pawn. It was destroyed almost immediately, and a white knight flickered into existence where it had been. Another pawn, another white piece. She probed carefully but with an eye on the clock. More and more white pieces flickered into existence on the chessboard and now they were moving, aggressively attacking her formation. She moved, rotating the sixfold board and flipping across the space between. She hadn't seen ice this aggressive in a long time. Since the War. It demolished her rig and wasted clock cycles as she rebooted necessary programs. She recognized some of the attacks; Deep Red was analyzing the data but she knew what it would tell her. They were pulsing information in the gamma range, specially tuned to create destructive interference with her brain's natural electrical activity. If one of these programs managed to tag her—and not just one of her pieces—it could kill her.

For Dad, who got me started.

Cover illustration by Magali Villeneuve.

Color insert writing by Jason Marker.

Color insert artwork by Antonio De Luca, David Griffith, Imaginary FS Pte Ltd, James Ives, Samuel Leung, Emilio Rodriguez, and Kirsten Zirngibl.

This is a work of fiction. The characters, incidents, and dialogue are drawn from the author's imagination and are not to be construed as real. Any resemblance to actual events or persons, living or dead, is entirely coincidental.

ISBN: 978-1-63344-222-1

Printed in the United States of America.

Fantasy Flight Games
1995 West County Road B2
Roseville, MN 55113
USA

Find out more about Fantasy Flight Games
and our many exciting worlds at
www.FantasyFlightGames.com

An

Novella

Monster Slayer

by Daniel Lovat Clark

Fantasy Flight Games

DAY 1

Reina stood in the center of an enormous chessboard rising above and around her. A grid of red and white squares encased her in all six directions, crowded with game pieces.

Hers were red, of course. The enemy's were white, moving in seemingly predictable, methodical patterns. She observed, and did nothing, as the pieces moved around her. *In a war of information, reconnaissance is an attack.*

Her body was elsewhere, unimportant—safe. Her consciousness was here, in an anonymous server in the midst of the NA Gateway Stacks: an otherwise boring and utilitarian data array whose meatspace location Reina didn't know. Its ping suggested it was somewhere in New Angeles—an unremarkable server in an unremarkable datafarm in the most data-rich and interconnected city in the world. Security through obscurity. Pure chance that she found it at all—an intercepted data packet from Gibson Polytech, Inc. had been routed to this very server.

If it's so unimportant and anonymous, why does it have so much ice? The board was swarming with white pieces: simple pawns with predictable movement, fast-moving bishops that swept across the board in complex patterns, and a handful of knights jumping around at random.

She understood that the chessboard, the game pieces, all of it was an abstraction. Her brain-machine interface and her console, Deep Red, were very sophisticated, and she had trained both them and her own mind to interpret Network data via the metaphor of a chess game. The pawns were submoron barrier ice, the most basic firewalls imaginable. The bishops were sentry ice, sweeping through local traffic in search of evidence of intrusion. The knights were destroyers, and good ones, with quantum-enabled random seeds that made their behavior unpredictable and could randomize her own rig if they caught her. Each chess piece was a representation of data, an avatar of a program, and their interactions were purely mechanical.

If she backed out of the simulation, she could read the behavior of the Network in its raw code. Thanks to years of experience and months of drill during her time in the Electronic Warfare Service, she could even understand that monolithic flood of data, analyze it, and—given time—find its weak point. This was better and faster, more intuitive. Here, in this simulation, she ruled as La Reina Roja, the Red Queen.

She sent her red pieces against the white, disrupting the patterns of their movement. A red pawn caught the attention of a bishop, which in turn called in a knight. The red pawn was a ghost—a phantom trace to nowhere, sacrificial and harmless. More red pawns were intercepted by more white bishops. A frenzy of white knights attacked enemies that didn't exist, and a hole opened in the server's defenses. She sent in a rook and the chessboard collapsed.

She was in.

And having gained access, was also at her most vulnerable.

A clear link shone from this anonymous server in the NA Gateway Stacks back to Brasilia Connectiva to the Near-Earth Hub to a Shadow Net server cluster in BosWash to DataMask in New Angeles to the network box on the corner near her squat, where Reina's illegal tap connected her to the Network. A good white hat could trace that connection back, given time, and find her.

This server's defenses had been good. Much better than she had expected. She set a timer, sending a mental signal through her BMI and into her skinsuit to terminate the connection in two minutes, the average reboot time for a defense grid like the one she'd just penetrated. Then she cut the time in half.

Within the server she found rack upon rack of data, thousands of files and directories stretching out around her in all directions. She sent out her crawlers and began pulling information down the connection.

A vast amount of data was its own form of security. It would take her the better part of a day to download the contents of this server, and she didn't have the time. Most of the data was junk—some of it actual garbage code, most of the rest good data of no interest to anyone outside of GPI's payroll department, or whatever subset of the company was using this server as storage. If she simply grabbed files indiscriminately, then in all likelihood the run would be wasted.

That's what the crawlers were for. They could analyze the metadata, the filenames and tags and keywords, and even skim through the files themselves for anything that matched their parameters. She had come to this server hoping to find evidence that GPI had concealed the dangers of brain-machine interfaces from the military during the War, and so her crawlers were tuned to find related data. Keywords like "soldier" or "veteran" or "casualty," as well as any reference to the prototype BMIs and related products that GPI had developed or sold during the War.

The crawlers flagged files for her as they went, processing far faster than any meat brain ever could. The blue orbs of data turned red each time a crawler marked it. Reina reached out to grab each red orb and pull it down into her console. She worked quickly, one eye on the clock, and soon had over ten zettabytes of data in her download queue—more than she could receive in the time limit she'd given herself. She dipped into the metadata herself, reaching out to touch each orb in turn. The halo surrounding each file unfolded into a wide pane, dense with filenames and histories and user-entered summaries. Her net had been too broad, perhaps—the first seemed to be a list of prospective clients for the GPI Mimir7 with analysis of sales techniques. She removed that file from her queue. The next was equally dry, a postmortem of a deal with Globalsec. She removed it. And the next. The fourth was a corporate memo from the Weyland Consortium, GPI's parent company, analyzing its strength in the marketplace. It was small and might have some value on the black market, so she left it in the queue. She found more and more files associated with the larger Weyland Consortium or one of its subsidiaries as she browsed. Most she removed. Some she left. The clock counted down.

The next file was labeled simply "Project Vulcan Threat Assessment, Feasibility, and Casualty Analysis." She'd never heard of Project Vulcan—some sort of new weapon? She examined the file in more detail. The file had come to the server almost three years ago—well after the end of the War—and was owned by a corporation labeled simply "GRNDL." She could find no more; the file was encrypted. She promoted it to the head of the queue and watched it download and ping complete.

She jacked out. There were ten seconds left on her clock.

Reina lay in the darkness of her squat—her base of operations, such as it was. She returned to her body in pieces, as she'd been trained. First, sound. The buzz and rush of hoppers outside, dulled by the thick concrete of the walls. She heard her own breathing. The drip of water from her makeshift plumbing. Then smell, the echoing damp cave-scent of her temporary home. She smelled a bitter tang of coffee and knew that she'd spent longer than she'd planned on this run. Then touch, her fingers running along the contours of her skinsuit and up to the port at the back of her neck. She pulled the plug connecting her console directly to the skinsuit and her BMI.

Vision came last as she straightened and opened her eyes. Even the dim light of her squat stabbed at her, and she blinked. She sat on a cot against one wall. Her console lay on the bare concrete floor at her feet. A workbench, nothing more than an old door resting on two sawhorses, and a dingy and scuffed barstool completed the workspace. Sheets of bioplas hung down, curtaining off her living area. She could make out the shape of a coffee maker resting on a desk through the plastic, the one comfort she made an effort to keep with her when she traveled. There was no sign of any enemy or other threat.

Reina stood. She sent a message to her console wirelessly via her skinsuit, instructing it to begin work on decrypting the Project

Vulcan file. Then she pressed through the gap in the bioplas, peeling the skinsuit off as she went.

By the time she had showered, drunk her first mug of coffee, dressed, and reheated a bowl of *mote pillo*, her console was done. An alert beacon hung in the air above its smooth silver case, directly over the luminescent queen chess piece logo. The logo was vanity, like her hair, like painting her skinsuit red, but it was also uniform. It was good for morale. Her morale, mainly.

She crossed back into her workspace and lifted the console to her bench. Unplugged, she used voice and gestural commands, and read its data off the holographic display it projected for her. The file was a multimedia report, aud and text and threedee all interspersed, of a sort commonly used in the halls of the corps. She set it to run as she ate. The default voice droned, anglo, boring— exactly what she'd expected.

"Project Vulcan's technical specifications and challenges having been previously mentioned and, in our consideration, solved, we proceed to discuss the social and economic impact of implementation of this program." A logo revolved before her, a red sphere with a lightning bolt running through it. "The immediate consideration is cost, both to GRNDL and the end user. Helium-3 fusion power and renewable solar sources remain both cheap and efficient. But as power needs increase, or if helium-3 production is disrupted, alternative energy sources will become competitive on price. Project Vulcan represents one part of a strategy to position GRNDL as a world leader in these alternative technologies in advance of their necessity. In short, we are ahead of the curve."

So not a weapon, she thought. She finished her *mote pillo*, washing it down with another mug of coffee. She pushed back through the bioplas to drain the rest of the pot.

"Still, the Board should recognize that profitability through traditional avenues remains years away." A musical cue reached her through the plastic. Reina could see that something dramatic was happening in the display above her console, something involving a rotating image of a structure. She crossed the floor to the gaps where windows might have once been planned, looking out at New Angeles, at the grey light filtering through the latticework of slidewalks and streets above her. "Furthermore, if the most alarmist reports from the geo team are proven correct, and the Vulcan procedure does create an earthquake cascade, civilian casualties in excess of ten million could result."

Reina stalked back toward the console, tearing her way through the sheeting. The holo was now showing a sort of schematic of the Earth's crust and a drilling platform. A pulsing red wave emanated from where the drill penetrated the mantle, then the image zoomed out to a map of the Pacific coast, pulsing red dots moving closer and closer to New Angeles. She presumed they were earthquakes. "The public relations fallout from such an event could far outstrip any profitability of the Vulcan platform itself, and such a setback, if not properly handled, could force the suspension of Geostrategic Research and Neothermal Development Laboratories' operations for years or even—" Reina waved her hand through the holo-image, cutting the voice short.

"Civilian casualties in excess of ten million," she said. She wondered how many civilians had died on Luna, on Mars, during the War. She still didn't know.

By 0700 she was on the streets, her console slung over her back, her skinsuit hung to self-clean and dry back in the squat. She felt naked without it, in rugged cargo pants, her boots, and her jacket worn over a thirdhand T-shirt. She was in Guayaquil, more than a dozen klicks from her current base of operations. It was better that way—harder for the enemy to track her.

It became harder and harder to identify the enemy as time went on. Reina was a servicewoman, trained by the military, but her mission was difficult to define since the War ended. At the time she'd been a staunch supporter of the U.S.-led efforts. But that had been before.

Now? Who could say. She was New Angelino born and raised, so her loyalties lay with New Angeles, and with her fellow veterans. People like Rafe.

Rafe was one of the founding members of the CEL, the Consejo para un Ecuador Libre. The CEL was a political group agitating for an early reversion of New Angeles to Ecuador, one of several groups that were openly hostile to United States involvement in

New Angeles. Reina didn't share their views entirely, but they were a useful tool. A weapon. And Rafe could be trusted. Always. Even after what had happened.

She paused at the corner. She'd come to Antiguo Guayaquil, where street level and ground level were the same and the average age of the buildings around her was about one hundred years. Most were concrete boxes, three or four stories tall, clinging to the slopes of the hill beneath her, their facades dimpled with recessed windows and studded with narrow balconies. Faded paint marked the riverside faces of each building, pink and blue and yellow. Once, Reina was certain, the neighborhood must have been charming. Now it was run down, old, in the shadow of the taller arcologies farther inland and the massive port structures downstream along the coast. It wasn't even fully wired—a thick bundle of cables passed from an overhead pole through the second-story window of a building to her left, the only obvious sign of Network connectivity she could see. Aside from a single NAPD camdrone hovering by, sweeping the nearly deserted street with mechanical indifference, no one was looking at her.

Safe. The enemy hadn't followed. She passed down the street to the CEL offices.

Two men loitered outside, Latino, like her. One of the men sat on an old folding chair, his mechanical legs looking thin and spindly below his ponderous gut. The other leaned against the cracked red paint of the building, smoking. Smoker was the younger, with a narrow, insolent face and bleached hair. Mech-Legs was the elder, his face pockmarked with age and scars. She towered above both men as she came to a halt before them.

"Rafe in?" she asked.

"Who wants to know?" sneered Smoker, in Spanish.

"Shut your hole," said Mech-Legs, also in Spanish. "You blind, boy? You see that scar?" She touched the scar on her face, noticed she was doing it, and pulled her hand away. "She's a veteran." He offered his hand. "Victor Allende Arroyo, Corporal in the Corps. How about you, soldier? You sexy?"

She took the hand and shook it. "No. EWS."

"EWS?" said Smoker. "That's no real kinda soldier. Soldiers fight with guns, like the SXC, not computers."

"Plenty of computers in the Space Expeditionary Corps," said Allende, waving the comment away.

"Is Rafe in?" she asked again.

"Don't mind my idiot nephew, here," said Allende. He struggled to his feet, his legs whirring in protest. "The closest he's ever been to real combat was the Clone Riots, and he was watching them on threedee."

"I don't mind," said Reina. "I'm here to talk to Rafe."

"This way."

Victor led her inside past a vacant and redundant reception area to where Rafe was working a rattling old printing press, running off genuine dead-tree pamphlets. Allende shouted something unheard over the din, and on the third attempt Rafe heard him and shut the machine down.

"La Reina Roja," he said, wiping ink from his hands. "Allende, you remember Reina? On Mars?"

"No, Rafe," said Allende. "Never met her before today."

"That's right," said Rafe. "I forgot."

"You don't usually remember you knew me on Mars," said Reina. She searched his face for any trace of the old Rafe, taking in his brown skin, the tight cap of curls on his head, the tiny creases at the corners of his eyes. He smiled.

"I guess I'm having a good day." He fingered a stack of pamphlets. "Victor, can you give us a minute?" Allende nodded and backed out.

"Do you remember my other name?" she asked.

He shook his head. "Just you and Mars. Red and red, right?" He sat on a creaky old stool and waved her to a seat. Her hair hadn't been red on Mars, she hadn't been the Red Queen on Mars, her skinsuit hadn't even been red. He didn't remember her. His brain was inventing a memory to fill in the gap. "I don't know. Did I know you back then? Or am I getting mixed up again?" The hope she'd felt growing died, like all the times before. She wished it bothered her more than it did, wished it hurt more.

"I have something for you," she said. She unslung her console from around her shoulders and placed it on a chair. With a gesture she brought up the holo-interface and spun through a forest of icons to the GRNDL file. She touched it and it bloomed to life. Deep Red confirmed her ID, giving her access to this file—but it stalled out when it detected Rafe in the room. She touched another icon, giving Rafe temporary access, and the file resumed its playback.

"GRNDL," Rafe said as the playback began. "I've heard of them, I think." Then he lapsed into silence, his smile vanishing. Rafe the man with the printing press faded. Sergeant José Rafael Cruz, SXC, returned, just for a moment. When it was done, he swore. "Jesus Christ and all the saints."

"Can you use this?" Reina asked.

"I can," he said. "Ten million? For no profits? This is what Victor lost his legs to protect?"

"GRNDL are the enemy," Reina said. "They're attacking our people. We were trained for this."

"And we're going to do something about it," Rafe agreed. "Give me a copy of that file. I can leak it to some nosies. If we can blow it open before this Project Vulcan happens, maybe GRNDL will back down." He ran a hand over his skull, barely disturbing his tight curls. "Ten million. God, I hope they back down. I wish I understood what exactly this thing is."

"Some sort of drilling platform," Reina said. "I don't know more than that. Need to do more research."

"Yeah," said Rafe. "Listen, you should talk to Tallie." He reached into his pocket and pulled out his PAD, a clunky older model about the size of a pack of cigarettes. He fumbled with it, frowning, and she remembered him on Mars, so confident and competent, always smiling, and her heart broke. She ignored it. "Contact card, Tallie Perrault. Send." The PAD's virt bloomed briefly in blues. Reina caught a brief glimpse of an anglo woman's face, conservative business dress, and then her console buzzed as Deep Red received the card and stored it away.

"Who's Tallie?" she asked.

"She's an ally. Some sorta lawyer or nosie or something working for a group called Opticon."

"Opticon Foundation," said Reina.

"Yeah, that's them. Do-gooders. They're anti-corp. Tallie talked to me about..." He trailed off, pointing at his head and smiling. "You know. My problem, and the VA, and the War. I heard she's been digging into GRNDL. Figure it's as good a place as any to start for you."

"Yes," said Reina. She turned to go.

"Yeah, good to see you, too," said Rafe. "Still need that file!"

She sent the file, and left.

By 0900 she was back in her work clothes, skinsuit under her jacket, console hanging in the small of her back. She stood out in the crowd, between her height, her red hair with its streak, and the skinsuit, but it was New Angeles. She wasn't the weirdest person in the plaza.

The plaza was just outside of Rutherford, an elevated square suspended above the network of tube-levs, underpasses, and walkways for the lower classes. Standing on the L-square, surrounded by slidewalks and carefully placed ark facades, Reina had the illusion she was at ground level. She knew that wasn't true, that there were a hundred meters or more of undercity beneath her.

The square was a bustling plaza crowded with suits, heavily anglo with a smattering of Nipponese and Southeast Asian. Clones and New Angelino service industry workers staffed the scattering of food carts and the lone YucaBean kiosk. A staffed booth instead of an autokiosk meant that there was money in the district.

Reina walked the perimeter of the square, tracking all the exits—the tube-lev station entrance, the six slidewalks leading away, the two hopper pads, the north and south arcology entrances, even the access hatches set into the L-square's surface, leading below to the tunnels. She also noted the troublemakers, the Human First protesters, the wylder kids looking for marks to chip-rip, the bored-looking NAPD officers watching the protest.

She picked up Perrault as she emerged from the tube-lev. She was shorter than Reina had expected, with straight blond hair and good shoulders and white skin. A swimmer, perhaps. Pretty enough, a normal anglo suit going about her normal anglo life. Her office building was a quick slidewalk away from here, so Reina moved quickly. She saw Perrault add herself to the queue at the YucaBean kiosk, and circled closer.

Then she paused, not knowing why. She drifted behind the Human First protesters, ignoring their chants, and watched.

Another suit had come up the tube-lev stairs behind Perrault, male, Latino, ex-military from his bearing. Active military, even.

A secman. He was feigning interest in the protest, same as Reina was. Perrault had a tail.

Reina considered. Why would a secman be tailing Perrault? Did Opticon have the resources to bodyguard their staff? Reina doubted it, and if so, why wouldn't this guy be right on her? No, the only answer that made sense was that he was the enemy, and he couldn't be allowed to observe her meeting with Perrault. *Knowledge is power, particularly knowledge denied to the enemy.*

The knot of Human First zealots clustered between her and the cops. The wylder kids couldn't care less. The L-square was heavily scrutinized by cameras and camdrones. She moved, circling the protest, keeping them between her and the cops. She sent a command to Deep Red to ping every camera that could see her. None had more than the factory-default security, so she instructed Deep Red to put them on loop. The one concern was a patrolling NAPD camdrone—crackable, but not worth the time or the risk. Instead, she faked an incident report and released it into the Network chatter. The drone's patrol algorithms would cause it to divert to check out the report, buying her at least sixty seconds. More than enough time.

She came up beside the secman.

"Nutjobs, right?" he said. "I think my favorite is 'Androids go home.' What does that even mean?" She'd approached in his blind spot, but he'd seen her anyway. She wondered if the opaque sunglasses he was wearing were projecting compressed 360, or if he was cybered for enhanced senses.

"I don't know," she said.

"Nice skinsuit," he said. "Saw drone operators wear it in the War. EWS?"

"Yes."

"Didn't think they'd let you keep it when you mustered out."

"They didn't," she said, and grabbed him on the upper arm. Her skinsuit pumped fifty kilovolts into him and he went limp. She caught him, holding him upright until she got him back to the tube-lev entrance. She lowered him to the ground, propped him against the railing, and straightened. One of the wylder kids was looking at her.

"That guy okay?" he asked. He had blue, furry ears, like a cat, flattened against his head.

"Just tired I guess," said Reina. "Don't rip his PAD or anything."
She left him there and told Deep Red to stop jamming the cameras.
The wylder kids would probably rob the secman blind. Good. Any
focus they pulled off her could only help.

She fell into step beside Perrault as she left the YucaBean booth.

"Ms. Perrault," she said. "Just smile at me like I'm an old friend
and you expect to see me."

"Um," said Perrault, and smiled a scared little smile. "Should I
expect to see you?"

"You can call me Reina," said Reina. "Rafe—Sergeant Cruz—
told me to talk to you."

"I haven't talked to Sergeant Cruz in…well, it's been a while."
Perrault took a sip of her coffee and looked behind her. *Amateur.*
"Shouldn't there be a scary guy in a suit and shades back there?"

"Not anymore. Don't look around. Keep walking with me."
They walked, Reina willing herself to slow down, Perrault scurry-
ing to keep up. "Tell me what you know about GRNDL."

"Grendel? Is that what this is about?" Perrault shook her
head and came to a stop. Reina turned to face her. They were too
exposed. The secman was the tail she'd seen; it was possible she'd
missed one. And in any case, he'd seen her. Every minute she spent
in the open talking to Perrault was a larger risk. "I'm done with
Grendel. I got the message when Mr. Scary Face dropped by for a
visit and my new friends started following me everywhere I went."

"Who is Mr. Scary Face?"

"He didn't give his name," said Perrault, shaking her head. She
drew a hand up above her head, signifying height. "He was tall.
And, you know, broad." Her hands flew out to her sides, her coffee
sloshing out of the cheap biodegradable cup. Reina resisted the
urge to grab Perrault's hands and make her focus. "He wore a suit
that probably cost my yearly salary, and sunglasses, you know, the
type that are really some sort of virt display. His face…" Her free
hand drifted to her face, tracing its contours. "It's like it was carved
from stone. Some sort of sharp, dangerous stone, like flint. Sharp
edges. Never smiled."

"Anglo? Black? Hair color? Give me more."

Perrault closed her eyes. Remembering, Reina hoped. "White.
Anglo or Latino, hard to tell. Dark hair, very neat, short, conservative."

"What did Mr. Stone say to you?"

"He talked around the issue a lot. Said a lot of words that meant if I kept digging into Grendel he'd kill me, only he never said the words Grendel, or kill." Perrault opened her eyes again, looking around.

"Don't look around," Reina said, steering her by the elbow. "Just keep walking to work." They walked and reached the slidewalk. The moving platforms caught their feet and they both came to a rest, letting the slidewalk do the work. "You keep calling it Grendel. Why?"

"Because GRNDL is a mouthful," said Perrault. "And because they're monsters."

Reina ran a quick Net search silently. Grendel: a famous monster from an old poem. She presumed this was some sort of journo-lawyer thing that made sense to college-educated anglos.

"You said you're done with Grendel. How far did you get before you finished?"

"Far enough to get their attention. Not far enough to publish. But I'm not going to share my research with you. I don't want to end up dead."

Deep Red pinged. It was done cracking into Perrault's PAD and ripping its contents.

"You don't have to," Reina said. "You've told me everything I need to know. Go to work. Today's a normal day." The slidewalk came up to a cross-walkway, leading to another L-square and a smaller arcology side entrance. Reina stepped off. Perrault kept going, her surprised face getting smaller and smaller as the slidewalk dragged her away.

She scurried against the flow of the slidewalk, scrambling past a tall woman with a cybered arm. "Stay out of it!" Perrault shouted. "Don't do anything stupid."

Reina walked away.

She took her time returning to base, wary of the enemy. She criss-crossed Rutherford and took the Skyway into Base de Cayambe before erasing herself from surveillance and dropping down into the tube-lev. It was after noon when she returned to the never-finished tower in Quinde.

Her base was on the thirtieth floor. She'd made it clear to the other squatters she wouldn't share, and regular payments to the building boss kept her plumbing working (after a fashion), her electric tap on-line, and her belongings secure.

When she got in, she did her routine security sweep and found nothing out of the ordinary. She peeled out of her skinsuit and plugged it in; stunning the secman had taken a lot of the juice out of her batteries. While the suit could function for days without recharge, she'd rather it be topped off in case she had to do it a few more times. She felt safer when all her equipment was in working order—the enemy could find her at any time. While it charged, she packed away the supplies she had gathered on her trip through the city and set her console back on the workbench to review Perrault's files.

The files were barely encrypted and Perrault's PAD had been relatively easy to rip. Reina wondered if GRNDL—if Grendel— had spiked the data with some sort of tracker. It's what she would have done. She sandboxed the files on a spare rig, wiped them off Deep Red, and cut off the spare's wireless. Then she began to review the data.

Most of it was either over her head or below her interest, which was to be expected. Financial reports, tech summaries, corporate minutia so boring and irrelevant as to grind a lesser woman's soul to ash. She reviewed every file, combing through for anything to use against the enemy. She found nothing; the most interesting piece was a personnel list. CEO John Morris. CFO Lupe Aizaga. Hector Gajula, Geologist. Juan Lee, Engineer. If nothing else, such a list gave her a name to put the squeeze on, but that was an unnecessarily risky move at this stage.

Reina tore the files apart and looked at the metadata. Provenance, origin, path through the Network for each file. Some were public, files Perrault could simply access and download. Others seemed to have been located on more secure servers, which suggested Perrault was either a runner herself, had a runner friend, or had a contact inside GRNDL. Reina identified seven unique servers of interest that she could pinpoint and took those Network addresses out onto a memory tab, which she transferred back to Deep Red. She put each address into a search crawler and sent it out through a Shadow Net anonymizer, and then walked away to let them work. Her skinsuit was charged and cleaned. She took a brief shower and slipped the skinsuit back on.

The Shadow Net was reasonably well informed on five of her seven servers—they were civilian-grade leasable storage units, some in New Angeles, others elsewhere on Earth. Easily cracked if she wanted to, but unlikely to contain anything of much interest. The sixth was an up-Stalk datafortress probably located somewhere on Midway and much more heavily iced. That, Reina decided, was probably where the corp kept its financial and other private data—employee records, perhaps. Worth a look. But the seventh was the most interesting, in that her crawler never came back. That meant it had run afoul of some ice and self-destructed rather than allow a backtrace. Reina would have to run.

She made herself drink a liter of water and took care of her bodily needs. She set another glass of water and some glucose tabs on the crate by her cot, within easy reach if the run went too long. She did another security sweep and finally moved Deep Red to the floor by her cot. She lay down and closed her eyes. She sent a mental command to her skinsuit, which flashed the time in the corner of the blackness: 1315. She jacked in.

The world was gone. She rushed through blackness toward the growing lights of the Network and found herself floating just beneath the surface, seeing light streak and blur from server to server. She remembered swimming with her Papi from the old fishing boat, out in the Pacific, joking they'd float to the Galápagos. She moved past it. She reached out and broke the surface, flowing into the server.

Everyone saw the Network differently. They'd taught her that in training, during the War. The brain of each person in full immersion interpreted the rush of data in its own way. But the data coming in was the same, and she'd been trained to a standard. It was possible to change your perception—necessary, in fact, to get good at running, at navigating the Network and exploiting its systems. The chessboard metaphor was one of Reina's tools, as much a mental construct as a sophisticated suite of programs. She wasn't using it now.

Now she stood in the midst of a great hall, its sloping walls breached by pipes and conduits snaking every which way. Packets of light zipped in and out of the conduits, occasionally pausing to resolve themselves into generic blue orbs of data, orbited by halos of extensions and file flags. Others had unique icons, avatars scripted by their programmers. Viewing the Network this way, not enforcing her own framework over it, allowed most of those avatars to render. Some were users, as diverse and varied as humanity could manage. Others were secretaries, software agents with relatively sophisticated AI like her own crawlers, out on some mission or another.

She was jacked in to the closest router, the junction box not far from her squat. The users who passed through were mostly others from Quinde, her neighbors, off-grid Netcriminals, middle-class kids from the arcologies above her—no one of interest, in other words. The router was of no interest, either. She chose a destination and became a packet of light herself, streaking through a portal and down a chain from router to router to router, then through a code gate that parted when presented with her biometrics, and down into the Shadow Net.

The Shadow Net wasn't a single place, or a place at all. It was hidden, and varied, the last frontier in cyberspace, beyond the reach of governments and corps alike. Parts were built into the existing Network architecture, encrypted and hidden files and servers living right on the hardware the corps controlled. Other parts were ad-hoc, peer-to-peer clusters that were born, evolved, and died hour to hour. The corps were continually trying to find and co-opt the Shadow Net, which meant that it had to keep changing to stay out of reach. You had to be in the know to get in, to swap bullshit and tricks and information with the other right people. Reina was in the know. She was a Member.

From the Manta Shadow Net node she logged into Members Only. The chatspace was a more traditional VR environment and the overwhelming rush of data was muted here, datastreams limited to sight and sound. Today Members Only was a sort of nightclub in a forest from some part of the world Reina didn't recognize. Strings of bright lights hung between the trees. A jazz band played upon a stage formed from a single tree stump, environmental avatars not occupied by a human intelligence and probably noninteractive. Avatars clustered on fallen logs, groups of people chatting about the business. Reina found a group she recognized and walked—or rather sent her avatar through virtual space—to join them.

PSK's avatar was a small pink house cat with a ridiculous fish-bowl-like space helmet. "Reina! You're not wearing the dress I made you." PSK had sent Reina an avatar-skin that was an intricate dress patterned after the Red Queen from some interpretation or another of *Through the Looking Glass*. PSK had told her that, and told her exactly which one, and exactly what alterations she had made, in exhaustive and boring detail.

Reina was wearing the same avatar she always did: herself in her skinsuit, but without the scar. "No," she said. "I'm not."

"She's all business, Kitten," drawled El Lobo. He was wearing the avatar of a handsome Latino man in a fine suit. His cuff links were snarling wolfs' heads. He varied his avatar often enough that Reina suspected him of vanity, but his face stayed fairly constant. It was possible it was his real face. "You should relax, *Su Majestad*. It's not good to be so wound up all the time."

"I'm busy," she said. "I'm looking for a server." She called up the Network address she had and displayed it above her outstretched hand. Lobo leaned forward to read it. PSK groomed herself, her paws passing through the bubble-helmet as if it weren't there, feigning indifference.

"So what's the problem? You got the address," said Lobo.

"My crawler never came back."

"Ah," he said. "Sounds like you're looking for trouble, then. What's on the server?"

"I don't know. But I want in. I was hoping one of you knew something about it."

"Not for free," said Lobo. He flashed her a grin. "See? I can be all business, too."

"It's in an Amazonas black zone," said PSK. She delicately lowered her leg and stopped grooming herself. Her fur rippled into a sleek, glossy black, with a white heart-shaped mark on her forehead. "It's some sort of private-owned node that doesn't have to play nice with the public Network. There's a whole mess of servers in there; I cracked one last year and burned it to the ground."

"A little extreme," murmured Lobo.

"They were big poopyheads!" PSK's tail lashed.

"It's like the Shadow Net for corps?" asked Reina.

"Yeah, I guess so," said PSK. "Free-roaming ice programs, a

gateway at the node portal, it's spooky stuff. I'll let you peek at my records, but they're super out of date."

"Better than nothing," said Reina. "What's your price?"

Somehow, the cat managed to smirk. "Wear the dress."

PSK's data was eight months old but comprehensive. Reina spent a few hours studying it, poring through the data—first in full-immersion, and then returning to her body to review in virt. She couldn't use the same techniques as PSK—there wouldn't be a sysop alive who'd leave security unchanged eight months after a penetration by a runner as vulgar and obvious as Princess Space Kitten. But the new security was likely built on the framework of the old. She dispatched a new set of crawlers to probe the limits of the black zone, and stepped away.

Reina did her exercises, thinking, planning. She did another security sweep. When she was done, her crawlers were back. She had a map of the terrain. She had intelligence. She had a plan.

Reina jacked in.

Concentric golden rings rotating around one another surrounded the gate to the black zone. All the gate did, according to PSK's notes, was log traffic in and out of the zone. Reina had already bounced her signal and hidden her backtrace, so the log would show her as accessing from an innocuous node near the Jack Weyland Arcology in New Angeles. She edited her ID, pulling up a clean persona from her tool kit—some suit she'd ripped weeks ago—then went through. Golden light washed over her briefly, then nothing. The gate didn't care.

The black zone within really was black. Silent monoliths, dark servers transmitting nothing, stood in rank upon rank. No traffic, no gleaming spheres of data, disturbed the stillness. She moved quickly toward the GRNDL server, alert for the patrolling programs detailed in PSK's notes. When she reached it, she created a pawn and sent it marching forward. It was obliterated almost instantly.

Reina pulled up PSK's map and studied. The patrolling programs were predictable but dangerous. When they found her, they would begin a backtrace, and when they traced her past the Jack Weyland Arcology node, they would realize her credentials didn't match what she'd flashed at the gate. That's when things could get deadly. She could move her connection to avoid the patrols, but she couldn't both move and break into the GRNDL server. Once she began her attack, she would be on a clock.

She waited, watched the pattern of the patrols darting from connection to connection. *More runners are killed by impatience than by its opposite.* The pattern had changed since PSK's run, which made sense. When she'd found her largest window, she returned to the GRNDL server and started the clock.

The chessboard rushed in from nowhere and the darkness of the black zone fell away. Her red pieces surrounded her, knights and rooks and bishops and pawns. There were no white pieces.

She advanced a pawn. It was destroyed almost immediately, and a white knight flickered into existence where it had been. Another pawn, another white piece. She probed carefully but with an eye on the clock. More and more white pieces flickered into existence on the chessboard and now they were moving, aggressively attacking her formation. She moved, rotating the sixfold board and flipping across the space between. She hadn't seen ice this aggressive in a long time. Since the War. It demolished her rig and wasted clock cycles as she rebooted necessary programs. She recognized some of the attacks; Deep Red was analyzing the data but she knew what it would tell her. They were pulsing information in the gamma range, specially tuned to create destructive interference with her brain's natural electrical activity. If one of these programs managed to tag her—and not just one of her pieces—it could kill her.

Deep Red pinged, its analysis complete. She pulled out a knight and modified its code, pasting in the exploit Deep Red had identified. It felt like she was reaching into the chess piece, changing machinery she couldn't see, and also it felt like she was writing code. Her brain was struggling to process everything Deep Red was throwing at her. She pushed on.

She sent the red knight against the white. It drew the ice out and waited for it to strike. The white knight sent a command to the server and the red knight inserted itself, sending a response. And again. And again. The white knight called the same function over and over, trapped in an endless loop until it collapsed. The red knight moved on to the next piece, and Reina moved again, past the white knights and deeper into the server.

An impenetrable wall of white pawns appeared, and then began to advance, serrating into a deadly pattern like sharp teeth. Reina sent in her rook, removing the back rank and sweeping forward. The ice destabilized, called a function and got no answer, and was defanged. She advanced again. This was aggressive play for her. It had to be. The clock was ticking down. More than half her time was gone.

Her rook derezzed and Deep Red informed her that hostile code had penetrated into its systems. From the pawns? Or another piece of ice she hadn't seen yet? It didn't matter. The code was contained, sandboxed into a dummy region of memory. She advanced and met the white king—the final barrier. It was tall, taller than the space within the sixfold chessboard, somehow. It was not purely white, but tinged with blue, as if made from actual water ice. It was perfectly smooth, featureless. Not dangerous in itself, she saw— but it didn't have to be. The clock ticked down.

She sought an entrance. She scripted pawns, an endless loop of pawns, to surround the white king and advance, their round heads rattling ineffectually against the king's smooth surface in a tight ring. They found no opening—would find none, not in time. But there must be one, or else why have the server on the Network at all? That was the secret. There was no such thing as impenetrable ice, because all servers existed to allow access.

The clock ticked down. Reina pulled the white king down, acting on instinct, trusting that her subconscious was finding the pattern where her programs were failing. It sank deeper and deeper into the chessboard, the pawns still rattling ineffectually against its smooth white surface as it slid by. The crown came into view and Reina reached out and broke it off, not knowing or caring what specific interactions of code that movement signified. A hole was revealed within, and she picked a pawn bodily from the chessboard and tossed it inside. It pinged back success. She was in.

The chessboard exploded as she rushed to find the files. The clock was still ticking, and she had only a few seconds to pull down the data she wanted. She readied her crawlers, already loaded with search terms, and stopped.

There was only one file. It was enormous. It filled nearly the entirety of the huge, echoing space. Another piece of ice, in its own way, she realized. All the data on the server, collected into its own nonstandard archive system? Or was there genuinely a single file of this size? She couldn't imagine what a file that large could be, unless it were some sort of AI. She had no time. She had no choice. She began the download.

The patrol program caught her avatar and began the backtrace. 5% complete.

The patrol program passed the Jack Weyland Arcology and red-flagged her connection as falsified. 7% complete.

The patrol program passed through the Brasilia Connectiva node and followed her link down toward the Shadow Net. 9% complete.

"End link, quiet mode," she said and Deep Red broke the connection. The echoing emptiness of the black zone derezzed and she found herself hanging in the soft red light of her neutral ready space inside Deep Red. She realized she was still wearing PSK's dress. She returned to her body.

Day 2

She woke early. First, she checked her security, walking her perimeter and querying her electronics surveillance. Nothing out of the ordinary. She had been vigilant about her backtrace, but still she didn't feel safe. She seldom did. She resolved to shift her base.

She hustled through her morning workout. She thought about skipping it, to see if Deep Red had finished decrypting the fragmentary file—but she would not give in to weakness. Her g-mods alone would not keep her strong. She focused, building a sheen of sweat as she ran up and down the stairs of the squat, pulled herself up on the bar, did her one-armed push-ups. She pushed herself harder for wanting to stop, and her body and lungs burned by the time she was done.

She filled her liter bottle and, drinking, sat cross-legged on the floor in front of Deep Red. Nothing. The decryption had failed. She finished the water bottle, then took a shower and packed. She took everything she couldn't replace, in case she couldn't return to this base, and climbed to the roof. A hopper waited there under a tarp. She'd stolen it six weeks ago and cracked its transmitters. It was red, Chinese-made, auto- and manual-switch enabled, and just like a million other hoppers in New Angeles. She couldn't remember who she'd stolen it from. It didn't matter—she needed it more. She loaded it up, making a second trip for the coffee maker. The refrigerator, most of the food, everything else would stay. She could replace it.

She wondered where she would settle tonight, and climbed into the hopper. It recognized her ID and opened its doors as she approached, closing them again as she settled into the seat. Her skinsuit synced wirelessly to its flight controls and she closed her eyes, jacking in to the hopper. She launched, threading her way between struts and animated billboards and into the skylanes, headed to Guayaquil.

She parked her hopper in a commercial bay at the edge of Antiguo Guayaquil. She walked the rest of the way to the CEL offices, doubling back twice to make sure she wasn't followed. It was just after 0700, but Rafe was an early riser. Maybe he would have an idea what to do with her impossible file fragment, or have a contact with a more powerful rig she could borrow. In the War, he'd been nearly as comfortable with technology as she'd been, pestering her with questions about electronic warfare and making friends with the tech staff on base. That had been before. Now he struggled to use his PAD.

She made herself stop thinking about Rafe, to stop thinking about why she was really here. She found the street deserted again, but this time Allende and Smoker weren't standing guard over the door. Reina knocked and waited. A kid ran by, kicking a *futbol*. A pair of stray dogs trotted down the street, saw Reina, and slunk away. She knocked again.

She tried the door. It was locked, but it was an old door on an old building, heavy wood with a simple lock. The door frame was wood, too. She gave it a push, letting her skinsuit enhance her strength, and the frame gave way. She pushed the door into the building and let it drop. The sharp clap echoed and died into silence. No virt secretary flickered on. The silence waited. She stepped inside.

Rafe's pamphlets lay stacked in their hundreds on a pair of tables in one room. The printing press lay cold. Stacks of binders and old dead-tree books crowded the shelves. Each rig in the back office was opened, its drive removed. There was no sign of anyone, anywhere.

"Rafe," she said. She started running, hitting the back door and knocking it out into the alley behind the offices. She sprinted up the hill, calling up Rafe's home address from Deep Red as she went. It wasn't far, just about a klick. She ran it in under three minutes, leaping over a parked groundcar and vaulting more than one dumpster on the way. Her skinsuit augmented all her movements, making her faster and stronger. She ran, knowing that she would be too late.

She found Rafe's house on the landward slope of the hill, a quiet neighborhood in the shadow of an L-square hung between two arcologies that thrust upward like mountains, their featureless plascrete bases sheer cliffs. An ancient stair ran down the hill, punctuated by quaint old electric lamps, half of which still threw dispirited light. The houses on either side of the staircase were low, painted in now-fading colors with red slate roofs. Dead or sickly plants and palm trees clustered in narrow gardens between each house and the stairs. Rafe's was the third house down. It had belonged to his father. Rafe couldn't have afforded a house, even in a crumbling slum like this, on his own.

The door was ajar and she crashed through it. Rafe wasn't there. She hustled through the rooms and found the back door, from the kitchen, open.

In the alley behind Rafe's house two bioroids placed Rafe's corpse into the trunk of a boxy black hopper. Rafe was wrapped in a carpet, but the rug did nothing to hide the familiar contours of his body.

Reina ran forward, grabbed the closest bioroid, and slammed it into the crumbling brick wall that was the far side of the alley. The bioroid was some sort of labor model, a Frank maybe, not one of the smart ones, but large and strong. And fast. It reached out and grabbed her wrist as she pulled away.

"Please, miss," the bioroid said. "I can't allow you to interfere."

The other bioroid was smaller, templated on the perfect average human male body she presumed. She recognized it as a PX, a versatile design popular with Martian pioneers and in space exploration. It tucked Rafe's body into the hopper and closed the trunk. It was getting away. Reina couldn't accept that.

The Frank pushed off from the wall, its big dumb face inert. It still had her trapped by the wrist. "I will take you away from here," the Frank said. It wore a tan jumpsuit with a logo stitched over the breast: Oceania Cleaners. She put her hand on its face and hit it with her electric stun charge. It let go of her wrist and grabbed its face, something in its humanlike brain responding to what it must have registered as pain. She hooked her foot behind its leg and shoved, and it tumbled back.

Reina had never fought a bioroid before, but it seemed to be a little like fighting a human. It was human shaped with humanlike limbs and joints, and it even seemed to feel some pain and respond like a human might. But fifty kilovolts should have dropped a human out of the fight completely. The Frank was already pulling itself back to its feet.

She had her own enhancements, both cybernetic and otherwise, but most of those were neural or sensory—her implanted brain-machine interface, her cybernetic eyes, her wired pain receptors. Her enhanced metabolism and immune system helped keep her fit, but she wasn't any stronger than any other human in her condition. She hoped the First Directive meant that the bioroid would do everything it could to keep her from harm.

She sprinted down the alley and punched the PX as hard as she could right where its kidney would have been if it were human. Pain lanced down her arm from knuckles to elbow. The PX reached back and gave her a gentle shove. She flew four meters through the air and hit the edge of a dumpster hard enough to knock the wind out of her.

"You could have hurt her," said the Frank, tromping to her side.

"Her skinsuit protects her," said the PX. "There was very little risk of injury."

The Frank picked her up. She smashed her forehead into its face, hit it twice in the gut. She would have done more damage punching a brick wall.

"Please, miss," the Frank said. "You might hurt yourself if you keep attacking me like that." It reached one arm around her and crushed her into a mighty bear-hug. "This is for your own protection, miss. I cannot allow a human to come to harm."

"What about Rafe?" she gasped, struggling to get her hands free.

"Who is Rafe?" asked the Frank. It tromped toward the hopper, where the PX still stood half in the driver's seat.

"She means the man in the trunk," said the PX.

"That man is already dead," said the Frank. "I checked. If he were not dead, I would call for medical assistance." The Frank came to a stop, standing near the trunk of the hopper. "Should we put her in the trunk, too?"

"The boss said no witnesses," said the PX. "If you put her in the trunk, she will be a witness."

"Oh," said the Frank. "That could cause her to come to harm. I should not do that."

"Put her in that dumpster," said the PX, "and put something heavy on the lid."

"I'm something heavy," said the Frank.

"The boss might need you," said the PX. "Find something else."

Reina braced her feet on the edge of the hopper's trunk, diverted power to her suit's legs, and shoved back and up. The Frank fell, taking her with it, and she managed to wriggle free. She leapt to her feet and jumped to the hopper as the PX dropped into the driver's seat and shut the door. The hopper grumbled forward as Reina scrambled to grab hold of the cab. She heard a *chunk* from behind her as the Frank grabbed on, too. The hopper rolled down the alley, the airspace above them not clear enough for launch. Reina didn't like her chances of holding on once it got airborne. She swung herself up over the trunk and kicked in the rear windshield with her power-boosted legs. The Frank grabbed her before she could get through the window.

"Miss, you can't be here," the Frank said. It almost sounded distressed, like a person. It hauled her back. "It isn't safe." The hopper picked up speed. As the chopper ran down the hill, the concrete and brick and fieldstone walls grew taller, streaking past in flickering blurs. Reina could hear the hopper's hoverfoils spinning up beneath her. She placed one hand under the Frank's chin, switched power to her skinsuit's arms, and pulled the Frank forward and to the side, scraping its head against the concrete walls. Synthskin tore like paper. Sparks flew. The Frank's face collapsed, its titanium and carbosteel-lattice skull crumpled and the top shorn away.

It didn't stop. Franks must have been one of the models with their brains inside their chests. "Please don't damage me, miss." Its voice sounded distorted, tinny—its mouth had been torn apart.

It was using a lower-quality speaker hidden somewhere else in its face or chest. Its hand tightened its grip on her shoulder and it pulled her closer. Its other hand was occupied, fingers sunk into and through the cheap outer shell of the vehicle, holding itself— and now her—steady on the streaking hopper.

Reina kicked its legs out from under it and they began to drag along the alley floor, kicking frantically in an effort to regain the hopper. "Miss, this is very dangerous! You might be hurt!"

"Tell your friend to stop the hopper."

"Stop the hopper!" The Frank's tiny voice was whipped away by the wind of their passage.

"He can't hear you. Use your wireless."

"I'm not wireless-enabled, miss," said the Frank. The hopper reached the end of the alley and turned, and Reina and the Frank were hurled hard to the left. She lost her grip on the hopper and scrambled to hold on to the Frank. The hopper began to lift off the ground and the Frank let go, twisting itself around to shelter her body as they fell and rolled across the trash-strewn street at the bottom of the hill. They came to rest at the base of one of the arcologies as the hopper vanished into the gloom above them.

A pair of NAPD camdrones came wailing down from above, red and blue lights flashing. Reina struggled to her feet. Her whole body hurt, but the Frank and her skinsuit had protected her. The Frank kicked feebly. Blue coolant leaked everywhere. The Frank's jumpsuit, stained dark with coolant and the grime of the street, was worn and torn in several places. She ripped the jumpsuit open and, directing most of the rest of her power reserves to her arms, tore open the Frank's chest. She found the parallel brain, a network of optical microcomputers like glowing blue threads, woven together into a simulation of a human brain. It was about the size of her two fists clenched side by side and the lights within each optical neuron were dying one by one. She reached in and shoved the optical brain aside, tearing delicate blue threads, until she could see the quantum processor, the traditional computer that worked in tandem with the neural lattice. It seemed to be little more than a black rectangle with wires running in and out, not that different from what she might find inside a high-end rig. She tore it free from its casing and fled, calling up Deep Red to purge nearby cameras as she went.

When she made it back to her hopper, she found that she was crying. She made herself not think about Rafe, not think about his laugh or the tiny crinkles at the edges of his eyes that came out when he smiled. She launched the hopper.

Everything was blackness. "Frank, wake up." The voice was dry, soft. She might call it pleasant, if she didn't know better. The room came into focus—the living room in Rafe's house. A Latino man in a fine suit, his eyes hidden behind black glasses, stood in front of her. He was peeling blue plastic gloves from his hands. His face looked like it was cut from stone, all hard angles and impassivity.

She could see Rafe sitting in the chair behind Mr. Stone, his hands tied together behind his back by a loop of plastic, his feet lashed to the legs of the chair. He and the chair were resting on a plastic sheet, which was specked with blood. The blood was dark and tacky; it had begun to dry.

She moved forward, carefully picking her way around Mr. Stone, and crouched down, reaching out to check Rafe's pulse. Her body, her hands, were huge, but she moved lightly. "Is this man hurt, Boss?" she asked. "We should call an ambulance if he's hurt." There was no pulse.

"He's not hurt, Frank, he's dead." Mr. Stone tossed the gloves onto the square of plastic. "Davy, wake up."

"I am awake, Boss." The PX came into view. She turned to watch as it inspected the scene from the doorway to the kitchen. "That man is dead."

"I don't know what to do," she said.

"Clean it up," said Mr. Stone. "Clean it all up, then take it all to the incinerator like I told you. Burn everything and then report back to me."

"And the hopper?" asked Davy.

"Clean it out when you're done," said Mr. Stone, from the front hall. "Thoroughly." The door clicked shut. Mr. Stone was gone.

"Okay," she said, climbing back to her feet. She lifted the chair, Rafe and all, in one hand.

"Not like that," said Davy. "Someone will see. Go find a rug."

She jacked out.

• • •

Reina didn't know how to crack a bioroid brain. She didn't know if it was possible. The best she'd been able to do with the Frank's drive was access a buffer of recent memories, apparently in queue to be transferred to long-term storage. It had only confirmed what she'd already known: Mr. Stone had tortured Rafe to death.

She didn't know why. Because Rafe had started sharing around the GRNDL files she'd given him? Because Perrault had talked to Rafe after her meeting with Reina? Because of the file fragment she'd found? What questions had Mr. Stone asked? The bioroid didn't know, couldn't have known. The First Directive meant that the bioroid couldn't have stood by while Mr. Stone murdered Rafe—he'd had his bioroids shut themselves down while he went to work. The Frank's first response on waking had been to try to save Rafe's life. The First Directive could be bent, evidently, as the PX—Davy—had bent it in her fight with the bioroids. But not broken. The Frank had died—had been destroyed—trying to save her.

"Soldiers die in war," she said, and disconnected the bioroid's brain from Deep Red.

"*Llapingachos*?" A plate of potato-and-cheese pancakes clattered to the counter in front of her. She looked into the bemused face of her father.

"Papi," she said. "You weren't supposed to find me back here."

"It's my restaurant, Maria," he said. He turned a plastic crate onto its side and sat on it. "I come into the back room from time to time."

She hadn't dared return to her base, but thought it best to get off the streets for a few hours. Her father's restaurant was in Antiguo Guayaquil, only a short hopper flight from Rafe's place. She'd landed her hopper at a pad nearby, one attached to a smaller, older arcology, and climbed down a long rattling metal stair to the old streets beneath before walking a klick to Papi's, doubling back twice to ensure no enemy was following. Now she was lurking in the storage room at the back of the building, where the delivery hoppers docked to unload.

She took the *llapingachos* and began to eat. They were hot and savory and tasted of childhood.

"You must be upset," he said. "You never visit anymore unless you're upset." He was smaller than in her memories, skinnier. The lines on his face were deeper. His hair was entirely grey. He sat in the same pose she remembered, legs splayed, leaning forward, hands resting on his knees. But now he felt like a miniature version of himself, a small man lost in the space of a big man.

She said nothing. He sighed and clapped his hands together in the air.

"Maria, come home. The War is over. You don't have to be a soldier anymore."

She remembered when she enlisted, remembered him begging her not to go. *"Soldiers die in war,"* he'd said. *"I do not want my little butterfly to die."* He'd still thought of her as a child. She still thought of him as a giant.

"The War didn't end," she said. "It only changed."

"You're chasing monsters, my little butterfly." She finished her *llapingachos* and he took her plate. "Monsters in the shadows." He reached out, touched her knee. "But there are no monsters. Just people. I don't want you to get hurt."

"You're wrong, Papi." She stood. "I shouldn't have come here. They could follow me. I put you in danger."

"Who's they? Why am I in danger? Maria, please, the implants they put in your brain, they've done something to you. Take them out. Put the soldier aside. The War is over! I haven't heard you laugh in fifteen years." He was standing, too. She had to look down to look him in the eye. She remembered the old house, on the Ecuador side of the river, the riot of colorful flowers and colorful butterflies, running, laughing, her enormous father calling "Mariposa! Mariposa!" as he tossed her into the air.

She ignored it.

"If the War is over," she said, "why do people keep getting killed?"

Day 3

Reina spent an entire day finding and fortifying a new base of operations. She settled on a place not far from the Rio Daule, one that overlooked a canal so choked with trash the neighborhood cats walked across it. The building was condemned—the entire neighborhood was condemned and marked for demolition. For gentrification. The only residents left were those too poor to find anyplace else. Reina had the entire building to herself, and the electricity still worked, although brown, foul-smelling sludge came out of the tap. They called the neighborhood "Rio Perdido."

She set herself up on the top floor, the fifth floor, and found a dingy flat with a slightly moldy mattress. The coffee maker was installed in a genuine kitchen, where it became the only appliance— even the cabinet doors had been removed. She found a chipped mug blazoned with a silhouette of the Root in the back of one cabinet, its handle broken off, and immediately filled it with coffee.

There was a bodega just at the end of the canal. She bought a cooler, a six-pack of *cedrón* cola, a selection of cup ramen, soy protein packs, six gallons of water, other necessities. The proprietor had an SXC tattoo on his left arm and the bleary eyes and broken veins of a broken man.

"Sexy?" she asked.

He nodded, then flicked a finger at her scar. "Luna?"

"Mars," she said. "EWS." She placed her scrip on the counter. The man took it and counted out her change. She left without another word.

She stashed her groceries back in the flat, and then took the hopper out into the next district, cleaned it, ditched it, and stole a new one—a nicer one, this time, on the theory its rich owner would care less. It was easy, far easier than compromising an enemy drone during the War. She parked the hopper in the little concrete courtyard in the center of the ring of apartment blocks, next to a rusting child's swing set, and covered it with the tarp again.

By sunset, she had set up her security and tapped into a nearby Network node. She was as safe as she was likely to get. She sat in the shadows of her living space, eating cup ramen and watching the lights fail to come on in Rio Perdido. In the other room, her console glowed redly as it chewed on the fragmentary file. She didn't expect any success.

She spent a few hours doing recon on the Network. She didn't let herself think about Rafe, didn't let herself think about Mr. Stone. She focused on the mission. Before she turned in, she cleaned, assembled, and test-fired a caseless submachine gun of Chinese manufacture. She slept with it by the bed, and each time she woke from unsettled dreams she reached out to touch its smooth, plastic case.

Day 4

She took the tube-lev to Punta San Lorenzo in Manta and walked a klick through pedestrian walkways lush with greenery only slightly tarnished by acid rain. She found her target not far from the coast, in the middle of a wide swath of industrial parks. It was a tall, blocky building with a stubby three-floor office annex and a series of enormous sliding doors facing a muster yard of heavy trucks and machinery. Its only ornamentation was five huge black letters running across the top of the building: GRNDL.

Reina found the closest junction box and jacked in. She went in noisy, smashing through ice and setting fire to the servers beyond. She didn't care about what files she was accessing, she simply set loose shredder programs to destroy everything and spent a few moments looking for the backup to delete that, too. She was backtraced almost immediately. She jacked out and blew a kiss to the camdrone hovering over her, then had Deep Red scramble it so hard it crashed.

She hiked back to the tube-lev, making no attempt to hide herself from the cameras. When she got there she found four NAPD officers waiting, two at the top of the stairs and two more coming at her from behind. She sent power to her legs and jumped from the street level up to the slidewalk above, catching the railing with her arms and hauling herself up. The NAPD cops shouted, two of the younger-looking ones sprinting for the closest slidewalk access, one of the others drawing her gun. Reina ran, and spoofed the cameras, and lost them.

The NAPD hadn't killed Rafe. She wanted Mr. Stone.

She tried again.

She found a suitable slum on the edge of Portoviejo and settled in a crumbling park with a concrete pool green with algae. She made a wireless link to a public access terminal at the edge of the park, cracked its filter controls, and jacked in.

During her recon she had found a public-facing Weyland Consortium site, a glorified advertisement for investors. It took her almost twenty minutes to crack it. She replaced the site with a scathing indictment of Weyland's business practices and world trade that she'd pulled from a public action blog and planted her signature, the red queen chess piece, right in the center.

As before, she made no attempt to hide her backtrace, and after jacking out she steadily climbed up the empty parking structure at the edge of the park. Camdrones began buzzing around the kiosk, fanning out. These camdrones weren't flashing the NAPD lights: they were black spheres about the size of her fist, made of super-lightweight polycarb and flying on vectored thrust through the air.

She jogged to the third floor of the garage and waited. The camdrones found her in a few minutes, the sec team not far behind. Three of them crunched across the concrete of the deserted, chipped, and decaying garage floor, two women and a man. One of the women, the one in front, was in a fine dark suit with a tan-colored coat. She wore the uniform black glasses and a PAD looped over her ear. The other two were in black combat dress, with armored vests and pads on knees and elbows. They had slugthrowers in their hands, solid dependable Argus-made models that could carry a wide variety of ammunition.

"Miss, would you come with us, please?" asked the woman in front. She was white, hair honey-blond, a little on the short side for sec work.

"I want to talk to your boss," said Reina.

"I can take you right to him," said Honey-Blond. She turned, extending her arm, asking Reina to walk with her. Her face was less inviting.

"I don't think you will," said Reina. "He kills people. He probably sent you to kill me."

"I can assure you that no one is here to kill anyone, miss. We'd just like to ask you some questions." Honey-Blond's expression hadn't changed yet. It was like her voice: clipped, businesslike.

"What if I refuse?"

Honey-Blond's face changed for the first time. She blew out a sigh. "Take her."

The rest of the sec team raised their guns and fired, faster than Reina expected, too fast to be natural. She twisted and dove for cover and felt a stinging slap against her shoulder and arm. Two cross-shaped stun rounds fell to the concrete, their charges spent and dissipated by her skinsuit. They each pumped three more rounds into her, hitting with some, missing with others, before Honey-Blond's shout stopped them.

"She's wearing armor. Switch to penetrating rounds."

Reina ducked behind a pillar, pulled the submachine gun from its place in the hollow of her back, and sent a short burst of fire across the garage. One of her slugs caught the armored secwoman in her leg, and the sec team scattered.

Reina ran, leapt, and crashed through the second-floor window of the apartment block ten meters away, landing and rolling in the stairwell. She kicked through the door into the hallway that ran the length of the block. It was crowded with discarded appliances, a bicycle, a woman carrying a basket of laundry. She screamed and dropped the laundry, and Reina kicked open the door to her right and hurled the woman inside. "Stay," said Reina.

Another door opened and a man looked out, two children wrapped around his legs. Reina brandished the submachine gun in his direction and he slammed the door. She could hear him shouting. "I'll call the cops! Call the Pistoleros! You get out of here!"

She sprinted the length of the block, hearing more shouting and doors opening behind her. She hit the door to the far stairwell hard enough to take it off its hinges, then swung herself feet-first through the next window and out into the air. She fell two stories, hit the street below, rolled, and came up running. As she rounded the next corner she saw a secman appear in the window. He raised his gun and fired once, a loud crack, and the concrete beyond her shoulder puffed as a bullet hit. *No more stun rounds.* She pulled out of sight.

She ran another ten minutes, twisting and turning and purging cameras as she went. She saw no evidence that the sec team had pursued beyond the apartment block.

She slowed to a walk and considered. Mr. Stone used bioroids. She wasn't sure why. Would bioroids have subroutines that forced them to report crimes? She didn't know. But if so, Mr. Stone had clearly found some way around them. If he did use only bioroids, Honey-Blond might legitimately have no idea who Mr. Stone was.

So, another failure. Her aggressive play had not brought out the enemy queen.

She made other attempts over the course of the day. She leaked the GRNDL file through the Shadow Net and gave it to Opticon. She attacked Weyland's personnel and payroll files from a café inside the public portions of the Jack Weyland Arcology. She found anti-cap blogs and fed them information detailing the Consortium's complex web of ownership and deniability. She scrambled the personal PADs of the CEOs of Bane's of London Finance and Insurance (easy); Gibson Polytech, Inc. (hard); and Argus Security (very hard), who were all in Rutherford for some sort of conference.

She made a point to let the security services see her. Sometimes the NAPD responded, and she evaded. Other times it was corporate security. In those cases, she evaded with slightly more aggressive tactics.

She saw Honey-Blond twice more over the course of the day. The first time Honey-Blond was still in the suit, flanked by security in carapace armor, but Reina stole a hopper and escaped.

The second time she had to identify Honey-Blond by her voice. The secwoman wore a hardsuit, not unlike the ones the SXC had used on Mars, her face hidden behind a centimeter of ceramics and steel. She braced herself in the open hatch of a lightly armored hopper while two of her team abseiled down from the other side.

"That's enough!" Honey-Blond's voice boomed through the

hardsuit's speakers, filling the echoing void of the Rutherford undercity as brightly as the floodlights burning from her hopper and pinning Reina in place. "I don't know what your problem is, lady, but you're coming with me."

Reina ran as the hardsuited sec team pounded after her. Anywhere she went, the floodlights followed, the hopper whining above her. She ran past a support pylon and the floodlight followed, the sec team right behind. She slid down a trash-slicked slope where the Andes buckled and fell beneath her, slipping under a highway thrumming with truck traffic, and the floodlight followed. She ran through a tunnel entrance set beneath the plascrete foundation of an arcology, a stream of autopiloted hoppers emerging and rising to the upper levels in a constant roar, and the floodlight followed.

Honey-Blond's voice followed, too. "Come quietly and I can guarantee your safety." Reina did not come quietly. "If you do not surrender, I will shoot you." Reina did not surrender.

A fountain of gas and exploding concrete erupted from the pillar before her—a hit from a laser or maser, the high energy superheating and vaporizing the material in its path. Honey-Blond sighted down the barrel of her weapon, daring Reina to keep running. Reina stopped and put her hands up. The hardsuited sec team approached, their guns leveled at her.

Reina jacked in. She overlaid Deep Red's ready space with sense feedback from the skinsuit, maintaining a once-removed connection to her body while she worked. In full-immersion, the real world moved slower. The sec team approached as if through tar. The hopper above floated stock-still, a piece of newsrag drifting in its backwash. She called up wireless connections, overlaying them as pulses of bright light on the visual feed. One pinged on each secman, two on Honey-Blond, another from within her hopper. Reina ignored these—they'd be heavily secured, and even if she could crack them the level of mischief she could work on military-spec hardware would be low. Instead, she shifted up above, to where the stream of autopiloted hoppers crept by. She pinged a handful and settled on an autocab that currently had no passengers.

To launch a wireless intrusion and override of a hopper or drone, Reina would first have to penetrate its ice and then interface with its OS and pilot programming. Every generation of every model of hopper or drone had a unique system, and no one could memorize them all. A good runner could slave a remote hopper or drone, given enough time for trial and error to learn how the target was controlled, but Reina had seconds, not hours.

Reina cracked the authentication and slaved the hopper to Deep Red in less than three seconds, replacing its OS and nav systems with her own. She would have been faster, but the pilot program she used was showing its age—it dated back to the War, when she used it to hijack enemy drones on the front lines. It had been designed by the military for exactly this purpose, and a civilian passenger hopper was no match. She settled her mind into the control seat and steered the hopper on a tight loop, and down, and straight through Honey-Blond's vehicle. The hydrogen fuel cells on board both hoppers exploded in a bright flash.

Reina jacked out, fighting through the disorientation that came from being a step outside her body. She was already moving as the sec team turned to shelter themselves from the explosion. She came up to the closer one and drove a power-enhanced fist into his faceplate, sending him stumbling back. She grabbed his arm, twisted, and directed the carbine in his grip at the second secman. She pushed, forcing his finger on the secure gene-locked trigger, and shot the second secman in the chest. He went down. She could hear the secman shouting inside his helmet, but could not make out the words. She grabbed the hardsuit right over its power source, tore the casing open, and pushed her stun charge up to the redline to fry its electronics. The suit locked up and she shoved the secman over like a discarded toy.

When she left, she could still hear him screaming.

When she returned to her base in Rio Perdido, Reina found that she had taken a bullet in the leg. Her skinsuit was already repairing itself, but the wound was angry and red and still oozing. Her g-mods had stopped the bleeding quickly and her implants had evidently shut off the pain, but Reina sat and broke out her medical kit. She dug out the bullet, sterilized the hole, and wrapped it. The pain was a dull burn. She ignored it.

After tending to that wound, she bathed as best she could and reheated a cup ramen with soy protein bars. She sat with her leg elevated in front of her console, eating and reviewing the Frank's video log. She found three good frames showing Mr. Stone's face clearly and Rafe's corpse in the background. She pulled them out into still threedee files, bundled them, and sent them to the NAPD, Opticon, the *New Angeles Sol*, and GRNDL. Then she unplugged, did her final security sweep at a limp, and went to bed. She slept slightly better.

Day 5

She woke to the shrieking of seagulls, and for a half moment she was back on the fishing boat with Papi. She made herself forget it, and sat up.

Her leg was still tender as she did her morning security sweep and workout, and she drank her coffee looking out over the trash-choked canal. A cat darted its way across the trash, sending a swarm of seagulls up into the air to call their displeasure. Poor as it was, Rio Perdido was still alive. Across the canal, Reina saw a woman shaking out a sheet from her apartment window. A baby hung from her hip, wrapped in a length of cloth in bright Quechua colors.

Reina finished her coffee and skimmed her Network feeds. She saw nothing about GRNDL, nothing about Mr. Stone. Nothing about Rafe's murder, only a mention that three members of the Consejo para un Ecuador Libre were missing, and that she had to dig up on a paranoid New World Order conspiracy blog. The *New Angeles Sol*, Opticon, and the NAPD had all sat on her video stills rather than run anything with them. She wished she were surprised.

Her own activities the previous day hadn't gone unnoticed. She had messages from both PSK and El Lobo, short text strings sent from untraceable accounts.

From PSK: "*I hope you wore the dress the entire time you tore them a new one. Nice work. Love and kisses, Princess Space Kitten.*"

And from El Lobo, in Spanish: "*What you're doing is completely crazy. What's the angle? I'm available for the next few days if the price is right.*"

She ignored both messages. She found a reference to a hopper crash that matched the time and location of the one she'd caused escaping from Honey-Blond. It mentioned one fatality, two injured. It didn't mention that the casualties were all corp mercs carrying lethal weapons to illegally kill or capture a New Angelino citizen. Reina wondered if Honey-Blond was the fatality but couldn't tell from the report.

Over breakfast she reviewed her prior research and Perrault's files, finding herself another target. She'd knocked a few GRNDL pieces off the board yesterday, she suspected. The queen would have to come out to slap her down. Or rook. Or whatever piece Mr. Stone was.

She found another Grendel facility, closer to the coast this time, out in the Guayaquil District near Salinas. Public records zoned it as an office and research facility, which suggested there might be some data there worth grabbing. The CEO, John Morris, had his office there. Blueprints showed it as a sort of mini-ark, only forty floors with no subbasement to speak of. It shimmered in the threedee, a tall bud or bubble. Rings and semicircles of rooms and offices clung to the inside of the transparent plascrete skin, arrayed around a central void. Swirls of empty space spiraled up the interior, breaking the rings of offices into subtowers like petals of a flower, leaving open space from the heart of the building out to the ocean beyond. Reina imagined it would be a fairly pleasant space to live or work in, as corp architecture went. There were even apartments on some of the floors.

She would go there in person. The run would have two objectives. First, to draw Mr. Stone into the open where she could take him down. Second, to find a link to Project Vulcan and a smoking gun of Grendel's reckless disregard for innocent life—proof that they had not just discussed the project, but built it. Neither objective could be achieved remotely. A file as damning as what she wanted would be hardline-segregated, on an internal network with no remote access. And she needed Mr. Stone to see her face.

Presumably Davy, the PX bioroid, had furnished him with her image, and she'd made sure the camdrones had seen her several times over the course of yesterday's operations.

She pulled more data off public records, cracked into City Hall's secure server for anything that was hidden, and put together a detailed schematic of the facility. It was called the Wong-Lopez building, and hadn't been built for GRNDL. The previous tenants had been a biotech firm and a consumer electronics reseller who had split the building and then folded one by one, gobbled up by more competitive corps. The Wong-Lopez building had actually sat vacant for a year, as had both arks adjacent to it. The entire area had been in danger of decaying into just another Guayaquil slum when GRNDL had bought up Wong-Lopez and a real estate developer had bought the other two. Apparently three billion dollars had already been spent renovating the vacant buildings.

Wong-Lopez was host to over one hundred individuals living in its apartments and another six to eight thousand employees and visitors on any given workday. Its Network infrastructure was maintained by SYNC, an NBN subsidiary and the biggest Network provider in New Angeles.

Reina put on her skinsuit and uncovered the hopper. She had a SYNC maintenance tech jumpsuit among her supplies. She loaded its ID with her last clean SYNC identity and put it on. It did a reasonable job of hiding her skinsuit, and the cap covered her red-and-white hair. She loaded her other tools into its pockets and on the toolbelt that went with the outfit. The Chinese-made submachine gun was a harder proposition. It was a magnetic rail system with caseless ammunition, so it shouldn't flag any of the usual chem sniffers, but any secguard who got eyes on the thing would know it for what it was. She thought about hiding it under her jumpsuit, but it would show up on backscatter and be difficult to get to in a hurry.

She prowled the halls of the deserted apartments until she found an old-style metal toolbox, one with an insert tray. She lifted the tray, put in the collapsed gun, and closed the whole thing up. She decided it would do, if no one looked too closely.

She got into the hopper and set its autopilot for a pad near Wong-Lopez. On the way, she jacked in and planted a work order request for SYNC into the Wong-Lopez building system.

When she landed she jacked out and took stock. It was 0815. She looked at her reflection in the windshield and adjusted her outfit, tucking a fall of white hair back under the cap. She stepped away from the hopper and let the automated pad roll it into a chamber that closed and rumbled away. It would be stacked somewhere within the facility's depths and returned to her when the pad detected her ID again.

Wong-Lopez was maybe a half-klick away. An elevated slide-walk would have taken her directly, but she chose to rattle down the rusting steel stairs to ground level. This close to the coast, the undercity-overcity divide wasn't as stark. The sun peeked through the clouds and skyline to the east, and Reina could see that in the afternoon the neighborhood would be awash with direct sun, shining over the silver ocean. An explosion of lush greenery crawled over concrete walls and cracked open asphalt lots.

There was a small groundtruck nearby that was gaily painted in yellow and blue and red, and selling soybeef tacos. A gaggle of young boys sprinted past her toward the ocean, barefoot, laughing. Two young women crouched on a broken wall, whispering and giggling out at the ocean. A man jogged past with a scruffy dog at his heels. There was more traffic than she expected. The people mostly walked with confidence, too, none of the furtive darting from shadow to shadow, the fear of streetbangers that she often saw from *disenfrancistos* in the undercity.

From here she could see the Wong-Lopez building, glowing like a lightbulb over the whole neighborhood. A broad highway and slide-walk system ran overhead, leading to Wong-Lopez and its two neighbors. Between the three hung an L-square—more of an elevated triangle, she supposed—that seemed utterly vacant in comparison to the bustling undercity. The other two arcologies were dark, broken, and empty, but several shorter, more vibrant buildings crowded around their bases. She saw an apartment block, fronted by a string of shops and restaurants, and what looked like a groundcar dealership. People walked past, going about their day. Street vendors hawked wares. It was all so normal it felt like she'd just jacked out of a simulation of New Angeles and here was the real thing and she'd never seen it before.

Reina bought a soybeef taco even though she wasn't hungry. She nodded down the coast. "Tell me about those arcologies."

The taco chef had the gift of chatting while she cooked. "Oh, a little ristie-versus-common-man love story, *querida*." She was a smiling, broad, and rounded black woman, her heavy arms marked with bright luminescent tattoos that spoke of a hipper and more dangerous youth. "Real estate developers want to knock them down, knock down the neighborhood, build much bigger arks. They think the reason these three didn't work out was they were too small. No 'critical mass.'"

"So where's the love story?" asked Reina as she accepted her taco.

"Neighborhood love, *bonita*. We got together, decided we wouldn't sell. Those big arks standing empty now, just a few *perdidos* making camp in the lower levels, *Deus salvá-los*." She leaned out of the window of her truck, *tsk tsking* at the arcologies, as if she could see the squatters from here.

"I heard the company put three billion dollars into them."

"I don't think they put three hundred dollars in," said the woman. "I seen no construction, not even patching the holes in the fence."

"Thanks for the taco." She took two bites as she walked away. Not as good as her Papi's food. She made herself finish it—she didn't know the next time she'd get a chance to eat.

She walked the rest of the way to the Wong-Lopez building, thinking. Was there any significance to the location? What about the lack of renovation? Did it have anything to do with Project Vulcan? *Observe and understand.*

Only she didn't understand. She wished Rafe were there. She reached the base of the arcology and saw no entrance. She doubled back and found a stair up to the slidewalk level, and reached the public entrance that way.

The front doors hissed open as she approached and she strode into a tall, blandly attractive lobby. A pair of palm trees grew in planters on either side of the door, ringed by cushy chairs and benches. The back wall was bricks of stone, with the letters GRNDL in white plastic at the top. There was some discoloration of the stones, the ghost of whatever logo had hung there previously. The GRNDL letters seemed out of place. Stark. Functional. At odds with the relentless pleasantry of the rest of the building.

The counter was manned by a hologram, an AI secretary. As

she got closer Reina saw it toggle its avatar from a twentysome-thing blond anglo woman to a twentysomething dark-haired Latino man. She wondered how it handled crowds, but she was the only person in the lobby.

"Welcome to the Wong-Lopez offices of Geostrategic Research and Neothermal Development Laboratories. How may I help you?"

"I'm Katerina Petrov with SYNC," she said. "You're expecting me."

"Of course, Ms. Petrov. Please proceed to the door on your right." The secretary flashed a winning smile. Reina proceeded to the door on her right.

There she found a backscatter scanner and a bioroid in a bland suit that stood guard over a bank of elevators. "The building is closed, Ms. Petrov," said the bioroid.

"I have an appointment," said Reina. "Your secretary just told me to come through."

"But the building is closed today," said the bioroid. "Let me check." She assumed it checked, using its own wireless connection. To her eyes, it simply stood quietly in front of her.

"It's regular maintenance," she said. "It doesn't matter that no one's here. I can do the job, get out, and be on to my next site." She reached into her toolbox. "Look, I'll show you."

The bioroid must have found her face on its blacklist. It stepped forward, reaching out with one hand to detain her. "Ms. Petrov, I'll need you to come with me." She shot it, a long rattling burst of bullets through its chest and up, into its face. The gun's action was almost soundless, its magnetic acceleration little more than a gentle hum and a click as each bullet slid into position. The roar came from the bullets tearing through the sound barrier as they left the barrel.

The bioroid fell back, its suit in tatters and blue coolant leaking on the floor. It tried to get back up and she shot it twice more with controlled bursts through its skull and the center of its torso—the two most likely places its brain was stored.

Reina's hearing came echoing back. She heard no alarm klax-ons, no rushing feet. She called up Deep Red, nestled hard against her skinsuit in the small of her back. The cameras weren't wireless-capable, which made sense, so she found a network junction box, pulled a wireless adapter port from her toolbelt, and plugged it in. It didn't take her long to crack the cameras and the elevators. She set up a secretary to edit her out of camera footage and sent a digital ghost of herself up the elevators, a decoy to draw security away. She took the stairs, keeping the gun in hand.

After the first flight she stumbled and dropped to a knee, bracing herself on the railing. The building swayed beneath her, then stopped. She stood, and continued, not sure if it had been an earthquake or heavy construction machinery working on one of the nearby arcologies.

Three floors up, she had reached the limits of her probe's reliable wireless range, so she stepped cautiously out of the stairwell. A cluster of hallways surrounded her, painted with animated paneling. G-modded plants sat along the walls at various intervals, a failed attempt at cheer and comfort. The central corridor led directly to the arching hollow at the center of the arcology, ending in a balcony overlooking a grandiose garden and waterfall.

She saw no one, human or bioroid. She chose a door at random and found a darkened office that flickered to life at her presence. An animated wall showed a beach. The desk was empty, marked only by a cluster of virt emitters. A shelf unit displayed a handful of knickknacks so bland and generic she wondered if they shipped with the shelf. One had apparently fallen and broken on the carpeted floor. There was no trace of the occupant, no hint that a human with a real life had ever claimed the space. The emptiness clawed at her. She ignored it.

She jacked in and set about compromising the building's security system as best she could. She was surprised to discover that her secretary was still in place editing camera feeds—a good sysop should have found and eliminated it by now. No sign of Mr. Stone. She pulled a building schematic down, and then her connection derezzed and she returned to her body. Deep Red informed her that wireless signals were jammed. The building was waking up, its security protocols gradually coming on-line.

She left the office and climbed. The building's datavault was ten floors up, roughly in the center of the arcology. Within would be servers that were not connected to the Network, not hackable from outside the vault itself. Any files damning to Grendel would be there. She would either run into Mr. Stone on the way or not.

She didn't. She did run into a pair of bioroids, identical to the one downstairs. She didn't recognize the model, but these were armed with Gandhi guns, Synap pistols designed to scramble her nervous system but do no lasting harm. They were fast, and accurate, and both squeezed off shots that made her teeth tingle and her body feel numb and prickly. Had she not been wearing the skinsuit, she imagined, or had her cybernetics and g-mods been of lower quality, that might have disabled her. She tore both bioroids apart with quick bursts from the submachine gun, and then hurled their bodies over the closest railing to shatter in the center of the garden.

She found the vault on the thirteenth floor in a glass room beneath a water feature. It seemed fragile—the opposite of secure—but as she placed semtex around the door, Reina could see the entirety of the vault, server trees standing in shadowed ranks. It would be impossible for anyone to enter the vault without being seen clearly by those outside for floors in any direction. A different sort of security: security through transparency. Odd, then, that the building was so empty. She blew the door and stepped in.

Water streamed down one wall, warping the light, making the room flicker. The walls on either side looked out over the central void, the vault projecting out into the heart of the building. She could see clear out of the arcology—through the void and through the outer skin, out along the coast—could see the city and the ocean stretching off forever, tall glimmering arcologies marching down to the flint-grey sea. From here the line between city and ocean was stark, although Reina knew that in New Angeles—as in many cities—there were arks that stood out among the waves, pushing back against the ocean.

She ignored the view and turned to the closest server tree. It was empty, each node that should contain a memory diamond a darkened hollow. So was the next one. A snake of power cables coiled, dead, by the back wall, and the terminals and dataports were missing. Millions of dollars of equipment that should have been in the room was not in the room.

She had secured the gun to her skinsuit, leaving the jumpsuit open for easy access, while placing her explosives. She drew it now and stalked carefully through the vault. She couldn't see how this could be a trap. Weyland hadn't had any warning that she was coming, not at this building in particular. Was every Weyland-owned arcology in the city abandoned? Were all their datavaults empty?

The wall facing the ocean shattered, an eruption of glass shards crashing into the vault and slashing across her face. She staggered back. A cascade of glass, or glass-like material at any rate, was falling from above, the outer skin of the arcology. A hopper hung in the blank grey sky, framed in the ragged hole. She blinked twice, her cyberware zooming in on the distant hopper. It was a bulky model favored by security agencies, its sliding side door open and Mr. Stone braced in the hatch with a rifle longer than he was tall. He was lining up a second shot.

Reina sprinted for the door, her wounded leg giving out and stumbling. The stumble saved her life, and the second bullet punched a hole the size of her palm in the floor inches from her hand. She scrambled forward on hands and knees, into the hallway, and hurled herself away from the garden, deeper into the building. She reached for her gun, to return fire, to do something, anything, but it wasn't there. A third shot bore a tunnel through the floors above and below her, punching through who knows how many walls along the way. It tore her SYNC jumsuit and grazed along the top of her skinsuit, knocking her back.

The enormity of her error felt like a shock straight to her bones, running through her entire body. Why had it never occurred to her that Mr. Stone would do something as simple and deadly as standing a kilometer away, using thermal imaging, seeing through the Wong-Lopez arcology's walls and shooting through them like they were paper with a rifle like the lance of god? She activated her skinsuit's thermal damping to mask her heat signature and kept running.

For a moment she could taste bile and remember shame. She ignored it.

She would crack his hopper, crash him, like she had done with Honey-Blond. She would climb to the roof and jump into his vehicle, throw him to the ocean below. She would find the building's security center and steal a gun from its weapon's locker. A dozen plans flashed through her as she crept through the building, keeping as many walls and floors between her and the assassin above as she could.

Her skinsuit cooled. Mr. Stone would need to find her with his own two eyes.

She circled the building and found herself standing in a cafeteria. A long counter stood hungry, deserted, and the long arch of the room was scattered with tables. The entire back wall was translucent, a lattice of interconnected triangles opening onto the ocean and New Angeles.

Something was wrong with the water.

Reina stepped forward, placing herself near the lunch counter and craning her neck to find Mr. Stone. His hopper was still above her, moving in a slow orbit around the arcology. He had lost her, but hadn't given up. She checked Deep Red—the signal jamming was still in effect, and she was electronically blind. Presumably Mr. Stone was immune, and was in communication with the building's bioroids right now.

But something was wrong with the water.

She looked down. The grey water had receded, exposing bare rock, sheets of sand, and tangles of submerged equipment. Reina had never seen anything like it before. For an instant she thought she was looking down at the surface of Mars. She could see the skeletons and corpses of buildings long since drowned by the sea level rise of the twenty-first century. She looked out to sea. The grey water extended to the uncertain horizon, where it faded into the grey sky. She placed her fingers against the skin of the building and felt, rather than heard, the alert klaxons wailing. It was a dim, gentle thrumming. Down below it would be a howl. Usually it meant a tornado, although they were rare in hilly New Angeles. Would the people who heard it even understand? Did she?

The water rose. The wave returned, breaking and crashing along the shore, and just when she was sure it had reached its limit and would fall back into the sea it burst over the beaches and up into the city. It rose and rose, continued inland, as casually and uneventfully as any other wave. Water rushed along behind like a river, a river that ran from the ocean and into New Angeles.

Hoppers and groundcars twirled and floated like a child's bath toys. Buildings lurched, then sagged and collapsed as if they were paper bags. She couldn't see any people, but they must have been there, fleeing, drowning, broken against the tide. She could blink twice and bring them into focus with her enhanced eyes, watch them die. She didn't.

The leading edge of the water, she could see, was now a crushing wall of debris, damming its own progress and then bursting free again step by step. The arcologies quickly became islands, tall spires with waves crashing about their bases. Reina wondered if any would fall. She wondered if the Wong-Lopez building would fall. Looking down she could see waves breaking against the skin of the building. She heard a great crash and wondered if the sea-facing windows had given in, if the garden below was now flooding.

Mr. Stone's hopper dropped down into view and she vaulted the cafeteria's lunch counter. The window exploded and the back wall ruptured and fell in tinkling cascades. Mr. Stone had changed guns, she could hear the chatter of an automatic weapon, see it take hungry bites from the edge of the lunch counter. She kicked open the door and found a kitchen. Mr. Stone was walking fire casually across the cafeteria and into the next room, seeming to cut the arcology in half. She sprinted through the kitchen and hit the next door, wondering how he was finding her. Was her secretary monitoring the cameras still in place? Or had someone finally switched it off at Mr. Stone's order?

Behind her she could hear the spangs and clangs as Mr. Stone's gun effortlessly demolished the kitchen. She burst through the door and caught herself just before she went over the railing beyond. She looked down some thirteen stories to the garden floor as the ocean poured in. Trees toppled, glass walls burst. It happened so slowly, so methodically. The ocean was simply scrubbing away everything, bit by bit.

Reina hurled herself over the railing and twisted, catching the edge of the floor as she fell past it and hanging in space. With the way the floors were arranged in their decorative swirl, the level below her was three meters away, not directly beneath her feet. If she fell, there was nothing between her and the incoming ocean. She swung once, twice to build momentum, and then hurled herself across the gap. She barely caught the floor in one hand, boosted her strength via the skinsuit, and pulled herself up to safety.

Her body was screaming in protest, her leg threatening to give up with every step. The spacious arcology interior echoed with the roar of gunfire and the tsunami. She didn't know what would collapse first: her or the building. She forced herself to her feet and ran. Deep Red still had no wireless connectivity, completely shut down by the noisemakers in the Wong-Lopez grid. She could break through it, find the right patterns of destructive interference to punch a signal through, maybe find whatever narrow part of the spectrum Mr. Stone was using, use any of her tricks from the War, but all of that would take time. Neither the tsunami nor Mr. Stone would wait.

She reached the far side of the staggered tower of floors, finding another gap, another pleasing void through which sunlight, seawater, and gunfire could filter. It was a good twenty meters to reach the next set of platforms, a gap she couldn't jump even with her skinsuit. On this side, however, the lower floors projected a few meters past the floors above. Two floors down was a bridge that connected the two units. She leapt, hit, and the building shifted. Every pane of glass in the infinite latticework that soared above and below her shattered. Some of the shards above were meters long, falling, spinning, as the bridge yawed and she slid. She dangled from the bridge by one arm ten stories above the raging wave. The hopper came into view, sidesliding and twisting to fix her in Mr. Stone's firing arc. Glass, like shards of ice, slashed at her, and a large fragment struck the bridge and burst, cutting her face, slashing through her skinsuit. Her grip gave way. She fell. Grey water rushed toward her, leaden, the color of bullets.

It was like returning to her body after a run in full-immersion. Her senses came back one at a time. First, sound. The cry of sea birds, the crash of waves. Distant, the grumble of hoppers and bleating of sirens. Someone wailing, their heart broken. She heard her own breathing, a coughing sputter. Then, smell. Salt water and seaweed, dead fish, the stench of the docks. An electric tang, like copper and blood. Then touch, sand on her cheek and in her mouth, gravel and broken rock beneath her, and pain, crushing, biting pain in every joint. Clammy wet clinging, sticking in hollows. Her hair, matted, hanging in her face.

Last was vision, which came back in stages. First, grey lightness. Then stabbing bright pain. When she could see properly, she doubted her eyes. A beach of rubble and slag arched into the middle distance. Gulls wobbled in the air above, calling. The sea lay and rolled as if nothing unusual had happened, perhaps a trifle browner than before. She could see no sign of Wong-Lopez or either of its sister arks.

After a few eternities she decided that she could move and discovered that she was wrong. Her attempt to rise left her rolling down the rubble away from the sea. New hurts joined the others, absurd in their demands when she had nothing left to give. She sat at the bottom of the pile, watching water pool in a hollow formed by an arch of plascrete. She realized she was staring into the dead silver eyes of a bioroid, buried in beams and shards of artificial stone. She had no idea whether it was alive or dead, active or destroyed. All she could see of it was its head and the stained and torn collar of its suit. She realized it was one of the Wong-Lopez security bioroids.

She tried again to stand, with more success, and found that one of her legs and one and a half of her arms still worked. Her left hand wouldn't close, not with any force, but she pulled herself up and out of the pit of broken things and stood atop the rubble, looking at the ruin of New Angeles around her.

"Civilian casualties in excess of ten million," she said. She staggered inland. Mr. Stone could shoot her now, or not, and she couldn't bring herself to care, but the War wasn't over and she had to get to safety. She wondered if Rio Perdido had survived. She wondered if she hadn't wasted a day moving her base—if she'd attacked Wong-Lopez a day earlier—if she could have found the evidence she needed to prevent the tsunami. She wondered if she could have saved Rafe's life by never bringing him the file. She wondered if every decision she'd ever made was wrong, if she should take her Papi's advice and give up the War. She wondered if her Papi was still alive, or if his restaurant was a pile of rubble, too.

After five minutes she found herself sitting atop the crushed hull of a Network public access terminal, staring at an overturned groundtruck. It was painted yellow and blue and red, and two dead people slumped in the cab. One of them had luminescent tattoos on her heavy brown arms, their light already fading. Reina could imagine how it happened, could imagine the truck driver stopping to let a passerby jump on, forfeiting her chance to escape in a failed attempt to save another. She'd seen such stupid heroism before in the War.

As she reached the edge of the tsunami zone, standing atop a mountain of rubble, she saw a mixture of bioroid models climbing up the slope toward her. A heavy labor Frank, wearing a thick jumpsuit with a Zona Sul logo stitched over its breast. A Jeeves, one of the classiest of personal assistant models. She normally saw them wearing subdued but extremely fine suits; this one had removed its suit coat and undershirt, stripped to the waist, its metal body gleaming in the weak sunlight, its flesh-like face and hands gentle and concerned. A pair of domestic GDS units, a handsome and helpful Brad, a courier model painted in bright corporate colors. The First Directive, she realized. These bioroids had dropped whatever they were doing and come to save human lives.

The Jeeves reached her first. "Excuse me, Ms. Petrov, I hope you'll forgive me for speaking out of turn, but you appear to be injured. Please, come with me, and I shall escort you to safety." It stepped forward, offering a hand. Her ID was still broadcasting, then. She realized that her console was missing.

She took the bioroid's hand and allowed it to walk her down the slope. Twice she nearly fell and the Jeeves saved her. The Jeeves walked her to a tent, apparently freshly erected, not far from the disaster zone. A pair of ambulance hoppers waited nearby, their lights pulsing, and a mixture of human and android emergency workers milled about.

"Here you are, miss," said the Jeeves. "They'll set you right. I must return and look for other survivors."

"Yes," she said, and the Jeeves bowed stiffly and left, slowly at first and then accelerating into a full sprint as its politeness protocols lost a battle to the First Directive.

The med-tech who collected her was human, an Asian woman in her late forties, she guessed. She appeared unmodded, checking the virt display of her hand-held PAD regularly as she poked and prodded and waved various instruments at Reina. She offered no false warmth or cheer, merely professional and clinical detachment.

"Your lacerations are mostly superficial, Ms. Petrov," the tech said. "The deepest one is on your left arm; it'll need sutures. Nasty puncture on your leg. Still, this skinsuit you're wearing probably saved your life."

"Yes," she said.

"Might be some internal damage." She shone a light in Reina's eyes. "You drowned, but didn't die, probably because of your g-mods. You should get a fresh brainmap at the hospital. Your brain is probably a mess."

"I've had worse," Reina said.

"There's an ambulance outside. Get in it." The tech packed her instruments away, clearly done with her.

"Other people need it more," Reina said. "I can walk."

"Don't be an idiot," the tech said. "You can share a ride with the other walking wounded." She stood and moved on.

The tent was abuzz with activity, dozens of androids and emergency workers tending to the injured who arrived in their own endless wave. Some went right into body bags. Others were surrounded by clusters of doctors and androids and machines. One confused man brought a bioroid torso with one arm and a smashed head and was sent away by an irate medtech. Several injured clones arrived and were treated when techs could be spared from human patients. No one was paying any attention to Reina where she sat on a high cot against one wall of the tent. She stood, wobbling slightly, and walked away. No one tried to stop her.

Without her console, Reina didn't try to steal a hopper. She took the tube-lev and endured the suspicious glares from other passengers. She couldn't even crack cameras, she realized. If Mr. Stone wanted to hunt her down, he could do it. She could only hope he was too busy dealing with the tsunami aftermath.

She bought a hat and a cheap rainslick at a kiosk with Katerina Petrov's ID and credaccount and wore them both. It would change her silhouette and hide her face and maybe foil most basic visual ID software that might be hunting her. It was the best she could manage.

It took her until sunset to reach Rio Perdido. The stairs up to her flat were too much to contemplate. She visited the bodega.

"Tsunami?" asked the SXC proprietor. She nodded. "Sit down." He pulled his stool around the counter. He held her hands, checked her pulse, did the basic medical once over, then nodded, rubbing his nose. He stood and wandered through the store for a minute. She was the only customer. She sat without moving, without thinking, and before long she was drinking fresh clean water and eating a hot soybeef burrito while the shopkeeper peeled an *orito* for her. She wolfed down the burrito, then the fruit, and felt better.

"Coffee," she said, just as the SXC man placed it in front of her. "Thank you," she said. "What do I owe you?"

"Nothing," he said.

"I'm going to get them," she said. "The ones who did this."

"Did what?" he asked. "It's a tsunami. Act of god."

She drank her coffee, and stood. She felt stronger. "They did this," she said. "Grendel." He said nothing. She wondered if she was talking to him, or to herself. "Thank you," she said.

She summited the stairs and peeled off her skinsuit. She had just enough energy left to hang it and plug it in to recharge and self-repair before she hurled herself into bed and slept.

DAY 6

She slept, but not well. Around midday, she woke with her bladder threatening to burst. She tended to that, took a sponge bath, ate a cup ramen, drank water, and changed all her bandages. Her wounds were healing—she healed fast. But every movement hurt and even lying in bed was agony. She couldn't even manage her security sweep. She lay down, not sleeping. Eventually, she stood again, staggered through her sweep, found a painkiller and a sleeping pill, and took them both with a swallow of water. She fell back into oblivion.

Day 7

She woke. A cat was shrieking outside. Perhaps it had slipped on the trash in the canal and fallen into the water. She sympathized. She sat up. It was morning. She tried to call up the time and remembered that Deep Red was somewhere in the Pacific Ocean. She stood, and found her leg much improved. She did her security sweep in a daze. She crossed into her work space and pulled out her backup console. It was smaller than her last one, a white rectangle about a finger's width deep and two hand-spans wide. The active light was blue. It had most of the same software loaded as Deep Red, some of the same mods—it would do, for now. She synced it with her skinsuit, then took it online while she attempted her morning workout. She managed the stairs once, a handful of push-ups, and her arms gave out quickly on the bar. She was exhausted already, her muscles complaining—the cut on her arm was deeper than she had thought.

She sat in front of her new console and waved her hand through the virt display, scrolling through messages and news reports. Everything was about the tsunami. An earthquake out at sea. One hundred thousand dead at least. One of the anti-cap blogs ranted about insurance payouts and Weyland-owned reconstruction contracts, and suddenly the empty arks made sense. Could a tsunami truly topple even a smaller, older arcology like Wong-Lopez? Reina didn't know, but she was certain that Grendel could make it look like it had, especially if it knew when the tsunami was coming. Three billion spent to do nothing in the sister arcologies? Accounting trickery, inflating the insurance claim.

The Members Only message threads were overfull, bursting with rumors, accusations, threats. It seemed that some were convinced that she had died, since she had gone dark around the same time as the tsunami. Another runner, StatiX, actually had perished. There was a memorial in Members Only scheduled for tonight New Angeles time. Reina had never met StatiX, and a rumor that she was dead could be helpful. She purged her access logs, leaving no trace she'd read the messages.

There was a single message from Papi. He was alive. He was worried about her. She reached out to touch it as it hung in the light of her virt display, then flicked it away unread, ignored.

There were an even dozen messages from Tallie Perrault, voice logs. She played them.

"Ms. Roja, it's Tallie Perrault. We need to talk about that thing we talked about before. Call me." Each was a slightly more urgent variation on the last. "Ms. Roja, Tallie again. Time is a factor. Things are changing. Call me." She skipped to the last one. "Oh god oh god, are you dead? Did he get you? Am I next? I have the silver bullet. I can bring them down. I need your help, and if I don't get it I'm dead and they get away with god-knows-how-many murders."

Reina ran a handful of anonymizers, routed her connection through Peru, up to SanSan, across the Pacific to NeoTokyo, off a satellite, and back to New Angeles. She called Perrault.

"Who is this?" Perrault's face materialized in virt above the new console. She looked haggard.

"It's me," said Reina. "You've been calling."

"Oh god you're not dead," said Perrault, hand going to her face. "Thank Christ."

"No," said Reina. "I'm not dead. Did you stop being afraid of Mr. Stone?"

"I'm still plenty afraid," said Perrault. "But they killed I-don't-even-know-how-many people. Maybe I'll be next, I don't know."

"You should go off-grid," said Reina.

"No," said Perrault. "I feel safer somewhere nice and public. Somewhere that if I die there, people will ask why. But that's not why I called you." She straightened, her eyes unfocusing briefly. Reina recognized the telltale signs of calling up data from an on-board source; she hadn't realized Perrault was wired. A memory diamond in her sternum, probably—a common mod. Reina had one like it. "I have a contact. A whistle-blower. He has enough dirt to not only bury Grendel in the court of public opinion but also to send people to jail. His name is—"

"No names," said Reina. "Not yet. Keep talking."

"Okay, well, my contact is in danger and he needs to be extracted before he'll talk. I don't have the resources. I was hoping maybe you do."

"Where is he?"

"That's the tricky part. He's on the platform."

"What platform?"

"The one out in the ocean. The one that caused—that allegedly caused—the earthquake. The one that triggered the tsunami." Reina stared at the screen. "It's at about one degree sixteen minutes north latitude, eighty-eight degrees forty-one minutes west longitude. Just about nine hundred klicks from the port at Manta." Reina continued staring. "Technically, my contact says there was an earthquake cascade, whatever that means, starting at the platform and making its way to the subduction fault at the edge of the Nazca—"

"Yes," she said. "I can extract him. I'm sending you a program. It's an encryption routine. Use it on your files then send them to me. Give me all his details, everything you have on this platform."

She sent the file and logged off. She stood and went to the window, looking out at the canal and up. The mountains rose above her, and the Beanstalk caught the sunlight as a shimmering thread in the distance.

Rio Perdido woke untouched. The tsunami hadn't reached this far inland. Millions of people in New Angeles—hundreds of millions of people—would have had no idea anything had happened, without the news, without someone telling them what to think. What would the media say about the tsunami? Was it like the bodega man had said, an act of god? She knew better. She and Perrault. And Grendel. She wasn't sure how it happened, didn't know the science. But she knew that Grendel had been drilling in the ocean and they had caused an earthquake. In fact, they'd known when it was going to happen. The Wong-Lopez building hadn't been carefully evacuated by accident. The fact that all those people who'd refused to sell their land had died—was that the motive? Or was it just one of a million small ways the Weyland Consortium had found to profit off a tragedy they had engineered?

She didn't know. And she didn't know exactly how the event would be spun, but she knew with a certainty that pulled at her like gravity that as far as the media was concerned, as far as the public would be concerned, no one would be to blame for the deaths of however many million the final butcher's bill would be. She should be outraged, spitting blood, heartbroken at all the deaths, angry that her father was almost one of them. But all she thought was: *The enemy is going to get away with it.*

She returned to her new console and found Perrault's files. The contact was Hector Gajula, and he was some sort of scientist. The platform was a Grendel drilling and research facility about 130 klicks from the Galápagos out in the Pacific. Getting there would be difficult. Getting Gajula out would be even harder.

She started packing.

Packing had been easy. She had no real idea what she was going to do, and in any case she'd lost most of her gear in the tsunami. She bathed, ate a tasteless meal of soy protein, put on the skinsuit, and gathered up her backup rig. She cracked its case and replaced its active light with a red LED, then sealed it back up. That and the full install of her program suite from a backup server was all she could manage. She shrugged into her jacket, only wincing a little. She was ready to go before 0800.

She had never recovered the hopper after the tsunami. Probably it had been destroyed in the flood. She walked out of the district and took the tube-lev south toward Guayaquil. It took her the entire trip to track down Allende. He was staying in a rental storage unit under his ex-wife's name.

When she reached his door, he looked like he'd seen a ghost.

"Hell no," he said in Spanish. "I'm not getting involved. You show up to talk to Rafe and he goes missing next day. What's going to happen to me, now, huh?"

"I need your help," said Reina. "I need a boat."

"So go get a boat. It's nothin' to do with me."

"I need someone who can drive it. I'm out of practice." Twenty years, give or take, since she'd steered her Papi's boat back from fishing, coming in to just kiss the old concrete wharf, the rubber tires cut in half and draped over the edge as bumpers.

"Find someone else."

"Your service record says you came into the Space Expeditionary Corps via the Marines, Corporal. You're rated on six different watercraft."

"Did my service record also say my legs got blown off by a goddamn Martian laser and I'm retired?"

"Who's that?" asked a voice and Smoker appeared over Allende's shoulder. "Not even, tío. We're in hiding, remember? No one home." He shoved past his uncle and stabbed a finger into her chest. She resisted the urge to break it. His bleached-blond bangs hung in his eyes as he did his best to glare at her. "You are one crazy bitch. You walk in and suddenly everything goes to hell. You leave us alone. How did you even find this place?"

"Time to stop hiding," said Reina. "I'm going after the man who killed Rafe."

"We don't want to hear it, you—"

"What do you mean, 'killed Rafe'?" Allende shifted on his whirring mechanical legs behind his nephew. She had his attention. "Who killed Rafe?" He leaned forward, bracing himself with one meaty hand on the door frame. For a moment Reina thought he would keep coming, topple forward and die on the floor. He ran a hand across his face, breathing hard.

"He's a Weyland Consortium cleaner who deals with their big trouble. Rafe was trouble. I aim to be bigger." She gestured and the virt display on her wrist bloomed to life, linked to the rig on her back. It showed Mr. Stone's face clearly, and Rafe's corpse. "That's him. He's the triggerman, covering up the deaths they caused with the tsunami."

"Uncle, he killed Rafe. He'll kill her—he'll kill you." Smoker's tough-guy teenage pride cracked. He sounded scared.

"He's dangerous," Reina agreed. "He's the enemy. And the War isn't over."

It took a little longer, Allende talking to his nephew in hushed tones, but then he came out of the storage unit and locked it behind him. "Okay," he said. "I'll drive your goddamn boat."

She stole them a hopper on the way out and jumped to a cache she'd kept not far from her old base in Quinde. It was in the tsunami zone, and it took her a few minutes of circling to recognize the spot. They touched down on a patch of sand and picked their way over to the basement of a building that had been completely demolished and washed away. A simple concrete slab marked its foundation, a pair of metal spars sticking up where posts once stood. She amped up her suit and pulled the big storm doors open, then triggered a light from her palm and led Allende down.

"What are we looking for here?" he asked. "Not gonna find a boat."

"No," she said. There was water on the floor, and they splashed through a dark mixture of ocean and oil and worse things. The footing was uncertain, with tools and debris hidden under the surface. Allende swore and nearly fell, catching himself on her shoulder. His mechanical legs wobbled.

The crates were against the far wall. A trickle of dirty seawater ran down over them, and she hauled each crate up to a dry place before opening it. A lot of the gear was damaged. But finally she found what she was looking for.

"Oh," said Allende when he saw them. She let him take his pick, and he pulled out and assembled an Argus assault rifle with variable ammunition selector, plus laser sight and a full optics suite. He'd used one like it in the War, she presumed. She found the ammunition, and he loaded a spectrum of armor piercing, HEAP, and hollow point, then sat down to load spare magazines. She left him to it; Allende clearly still knew his way around a firearm.

For herself she loaded a Neo Muscovite–made semi-automatic rifle with good range and penetration. Its electronics were suspect after being submerged, but the action of the weapon itself was purely mechanical and could survive far worse. She swapped out the electronics suite with another gun's and tested the connection from the grip through her skinsuit. It was good.

She pulled out another, smaller crate of sidearms and set Allende to assembling a selection of those as well. She went digging for her own supplies.

In the end, with all the water damage, she was able to salvage about six kilos of semtex and three drones: two basic civilian surveillance LAAVs only a little more robust and capable than a camdrone, and a highly restricted fifteen-year-old obsolete military Specter from the War.

The LAAVs looked something like a three-leaf clover, round rotor assemblages surrounding a black central body studded with camera blisters and sensors.

The Specter was larger and both looked and felt more deadly, its rotors hidden behind a sleek curving frame, painted a radar-invisible matte black like a dagger-shaped piece of midnight.

"You just had this crap down here all this time?" Allende asked as he laid out a selection of handguns.

"I've added to it over the years," she said. "Bought some, stole others. Still have some allies in the Service. Mostly it's more trouble than it's worth to carry one of these with you."

"So this time it's for serious." He nodded, and in the wavering light he looked grim and younger all at once. "We're gonna die, huh."

"Probably," she said.

"Well, let's take some of the *pendejos* with us."

They repacked the guns into one of the smaller crates, the drones and the explosives into another. Allende couldn't manage the footing and the stairs and a crate all at the same time on his legs, so she carried them both. Her arm didn't quite give out. The crates fit in the hopper's trunk.

"Do you have a boat?" Allende asked.

"Not yet," she said.

"Probably most of them got swamped," he said. "Maybe the ones that were out at sea are okay. Would they be? I don't know. Would they be sunk by the tidal wave?"

"No," she said, not really knowing. "There will be boats." She launched the hopper, angling up toward Manta. "How fast are these things?"

"Some fast, some slow. How far are we going?"

"About nine hundred klicks."

"...you better stop and get some food and water."

They stopped for food, water, and a solar converter.

They found a boat out in what was left of Manta tied up at the only usable wharf for klicks in any direction. It was a busy marina, crowds of waterproof-coveralled aquafarmers and other sailors mobbing the waterfront office. Androids were everywhere, crewing boats, carrying coolers of fish and shrimp, clearing wreckage and tending to damage. The risties were wisely absent, although it seemed that this had once been an expensive wharf for pleasure craft.

The boat Allende chose was a tall-cabined sport fisher with an inboard motor. Reina thought it looked like a fancier, richer, larger version of her Papi's old boat. The name written across the prow was *Princess Rosie*. "Really?" she said. "You're going to put the Red Queen on *Princess Rosie*?"

"Shut the hell up," said Allende. "This is the boat."

Reina found a clone wearing the marina's uniform and got his attention. "I want it refueled and ready to go in an hour, or I'll be talking to your boss. *Comprende*?" The clone stammered an answer and ran off, and Reina and Allende made two trips from the hopper to the boat to get all their gear stowed.

"Hey," said Allende. He held up a fancy deep-sea fishing rod. "We got stuff to do when we get bored."

"Can we fish at cruising speed?"

"Well, no, but—"

"Then no." She set the last crate down in the boat. "No breaks, no delays." She checked her console. "Wireless here is clogged. Infrastructure took a hit. Let me set up a satellite repeater."

Allende stowed gear and muttered something about "queen hard-ass" while Reina unpacked and deployed a satellite repeater to the roof of the cabin. Then she jacked in, found the registration for the *Princess Rosie*, and changed it to her name—or rather, the name of Charity Alvarez Feliciano, which was her latest clean ID. She left the billing information at the marina the same.

The clone came back ten minutes later with a stack of fuel cells on a cart. Allende worked with him to swap out the boat's old cells and signed a thumbs-up from the pilot's seat. The clone left and Reina untied from the wharf.

Allende threw the boat into gear and they chugged out to sea. "Can we go faster?" asked Reina.

"Not legally," he said. "Everyone's nice and careful close to shore so we don't hit each other. Also, there's a lot of bad things right there under the water after the goddamn wave." He gestured at an amber virt display flickering in the air before him. "See this? It's our sonar. There's enough crap down there I'm going to go nice and slow and careful and—'hup, hang on." He threw the boat into reverse and swung wide around something Reina couldn't see. She couldn't interpret the sonar display. "We'll open her up and see what this *puta* can do once we hit open water. Then it'll depend on the weather and seas."

Reina paced. She checked connectivity, paced again. She set up the solar converter and double-checked the power levels on all the drones. She packed it all away again. She resisted the urge to pull out the guns and check them—this close to shore, it would only call in unwanted attention.

Eventually, they made it out of the harbor and clear of the local shipping. Allende opened the throttle, and the boat started chuffing through the water, slapping each wave with a stomach-shaking *thump.*

"Ha!" he called. "Wonder what our top end is?" He accelerated.

Reina crowded into the cabin next to him. "Well?" she asked.

"We're doing sixty knots now," he said. "That's about…110 klicks per hour."

"That's good," she said.

"We won't be able to keep up this pace," he said. "Figure cruising is closer to forty or fifty knots, depending on the seas."

"What does that mean?"

"If the seas are high, that means taller waves, and we lose speed every time we hit a wave. We can't go the same speed on high seas that we can on a glass lake." The boat thump-thumped through the water. She could see that Allende was right. "So, where am I going?" She gave him the coordinates.

She climbed past the cabin and settled herself on a coil of rope on the bow. After a few minutes, Allende joined her.

"Autopilot's set," he said. "Should do the job unless we hit rough seas or the GPS cuts out. Figure we'll be there in about twelve hours."

"Perfect," she said. "It will be dark. Before we come over the horizon we'll want to cut all the lights and any transmissions."

"Sure," he said. "But it won't do any fragging good. This is some sorta big corp facility out in the middle of the goddamn ocean; they're going to have sonar and radar and crap. Mark-one eyeball is not the problem, here."

"Mark-one eyeball is the only one I can't crack," she said. "So you worry about that. I'll handle the others." She lay back, slid the port into her skull, and jacked in.

She spent about two hours doing the recon, the legwork, finding the Grendel servers, pulling down all the schematics and intelligence she could find. Unsurprisingly, the platform's physical security wasn't on the Network. She'd have to find another way to crack it. She overlaid data from the GPS and the *Princess Rosie's* pilot secretary and checked it against her Specter's maximum range. She left that link open and wrote a routine to alert her when the platform got close enough. She jacked out.

Hearing returned first, the thrum of the boat both heard and felt, the slap of the waves, the spray. Smell: the sea, strong and clean and clear. Touch: the rough deck beneath her fingertips, the wind tousling her hair. Vision was the bright warmth of an endless sky. She was a little girl again, out in Papi's boat south of Guayaquil, dozing in the sun. She ignored it.

She stood and picked her way back past the cabin. Allende was standing amidships, watching the Beanstalk vanish behind them. The rest of New Angeles was already below the horizon, and the Beanstalk was little more than a crease in the sky.

"In the War," he said, "we all did some things we're not proud of."

"Yes," she said.

"We lost friends. We killed. Sometimes…well, it's not like all the goddamn Loonies who died were soldiers, no?"

"No," she said.

Allende drummed his fingers on the gunwale. "But even at our crappiest, even the most deadly…it was never senseless. Never for no reason. The objective was always clear." He turned to her. "What was their objective? You're telling me they caused the wave. Why?"

"I don't know," she said. "We're going out there to find out."

"And get the guy who fragged Rafe?"

"And that. He killed to keep this secret once; he'll show up to do it again."

They rode in silence for a bit. Reina checked her map overlays. She had hours before the platform would be in range. Allende returned to the cabin and emerged a little later with a small white plastic box. It unfolded into a travel chess set. "Do you play?" he asked.

"Checkmate," she said again, moving her queen. The black queen, in this case. The chess set lacked any red pieces.

She turned her attention back to the drone laid out on the deck before her. She was making some adjustments to the laser communications suite attached to the LAAV's underside. A necessary aftermarket modification. She would turn the LAAVs into repeaters so she could keep line of sight for laser comms to the Specter while using it to break into the platform's own laser communications array.

Allende knocked his king over and huffed. "Crap," he said. "I guess you're pretty good." She'd beaten him five out of five games so far.

"Yes," she said.

"You ever lose?" he asked.

"Yes," she said. "I lose to top-tier players routinely." She paused, clenching and unclenching her hand on her injured arm. "We all lose sometimes."

"You're not going to give some boring lecture about how being good at chess makes you a master hacker?"

"No," she said. "If you're playing chess with the enemy, what's the best move?"

"No idea," he said. "Clearly."

"Draw your sidearm and shoot him in the head." She flipped the drone over. She flicked her fingers and sent a few gestural commands from the skinsuit through her console. The LAAV took off, hovered, spun in a slow circle. The balance was good. "Even the best players lose sometimes. So the best way to win is to cheat. That's one lesson to take from chess." She sent the drone back down the deck and packed it away.

"I dig it. The best way to fight is kick ass as hard as you can, any way you can. Anything less than that gets you dead."

"Right," she said. Allende set up the board again. "Chess is just a metaphor. It does train you to think ahead, to consider all the variables before you commit to a move."

"And did you? Consider the variables?" He took a black pawn and a white pawn, hid them in his hands, and held them out. She tapped the right hand, and got the black pawn again.

"Yes," she said.

"You thought it through and decided that the best move was to take a washed-up ex-Marine with you and attack an enemy base in a fishing boat." Allende moved his knight. "Sounds like we're desperate and have no other options."

She moved a pawn. "Yes."

"Gonna need some encouragement, here," he said, moving his other knight.

"Knights can be a strong opening," she said. She moved another pawn up to support her first.

"I meant about this crazy-ass mission, not about the game." He pursed his lips, studying the board, and realized her pawns had left his king's knight nowhere safe to go.

"Chess is a flawed metaphor for battle because chess is a game of perfect information." She gestured at the board. "You and I have the exact same knowledge of the board state. We perfectly understand one another's objectives. That does not happen in the real world. Information asymmetry is the norm in real combat, and knowing more than the enemy is how you win."

"Waiting for that encouragement." He moved his other knight.

"Mr. Stone probably thinks I died in the tsunami," she said. "If he's looking for you, he's doing it on the mainland. They have no reason to look for two desperadoes in a boat crossing nine hundred kilometers of ocean to attack them in their most remote facility." She moved her bishop.

"So what you're saying is…this is so stupid, it might just work?" He moved his knight.

She captured the knight.

She watched the sun set from the bow of the boat, sitting cross-legged as the day died in fire. The waves were high and their progress choppy, each spray of seawater erupting into a burning haze of red as the sunset filtered through. The red made her think of Mars, but Mars wasn't red, not really, more of a dusty orange. She remembered watching the sun set with Rafe, side by side in their envirosuits on the slopes of Pavonis Mons, the sun so small and weak and dim by comparison.

By the time the sun was a ruddy glow on the horizon, her console informed her that the platform was in range. She stood, made final adjustments to the portable laser comms array installed on the upper deck of the *Princess Rosie*, and launched the Specter. Then she went down into the cabin to talk to Allende.

"I'm going to start a run as soon as my drone gets in range," she said. "I'll be fully immersed. Keep my body secure."

"How do I wake your ass up if we capsize or something?" Allende was slurping noodles from a self-heating cup, sitting on the pilot's seat and keeping one eye on the controls.

"Reach inside my skinsuit and pull the jack out of my skull," she said. She held her hair up and pulled the skinsuit back to show him where it plugged into her body.

"Well, that's…horrifying," he said.

"You have robot legs."

"That's different. I lost my real legs in the War." He tapped one metal leg where it emerged from his cutoff shorts. "These pieces of junk are just the best I can do."

"Everyone lost something," she said, and grabbed a bottle of water and her own cup ramen. She drank, ate, then drank another bottle. "Probably best to clean the guns and get them ready while I'm under."

"Aye aye, Skipper," he said, and slurped his noodles.

She lay down on the deck and jacked in. From inside her ready space, she couldn't tell the difference between the new console and Deep Red. The secretary wasn't as fine-tuned, of course—hadn't had as much time to learn her quirks. She supposed she'd have to name it if she was going to keep it.

This far from shore, there was no question of connecting directly to the Network, no local wireless hub. She could activate the repeater and connect that way, beaming her signal up to a SYNC satellite in orbit and bouncing clear across Earth should she so desire. But doing that might let the Grendel security staff on the platform see her coming. So instead, she connected to the laser comms array and from there to her drone. The datastream between the boat and the drone was carried by a laser; the only way to intercept or even detect it was to physically get in the way. The swell of the waves and movement of the boat made the connection spotty, however. Sometimes she'd drop out for a full second as the drone and array scrambled to find each other again.

It wasn't perfect, but it should be enough. She began by loading the Specter's memory with her most important programs: weak-AI icebreakers, crawlers, programs that could continue to do their job if she lost connection. Then she sent the drone ahead and found Grendel's own laser array. It was pointed at the sky.

Once the drone was in place, it eavesdropped and sent traffic logs back to her console for analysis. She crunched them and figured out their comms protocols, which let her spoof them and use the Specter to start talking to the platform systems. After that, it was like any other run. The server's ice wasn't anything terribly impressive; it was nine hundred klicks from shore and of interest to practically no one. That was its true security.

Reina accessed the platform's security controls and found that it had already detected their boat. She installed a secretary and created a new script, inventing a path for the boat curving to the southwest and heading for the Galápagos. The platform would see that false path, oblivious to the boat's true movements. She wrote herself a back door for future intrusions, paying special attention to the platform's wireless intranet, and created a new superuser account for herself. When she was done, she owned the platform's security.

She jacked out and found Allende looking at her with a frown, his pockmarked face even more furrowed than normal.

"What?" she said.

"You looked sorta dead."

"I wasn't," she said. She stood. "Didn't you see raiders jack in during the War? Or rear-echelon drone pilots?"

"No," he said. "My unit never had an EWS embed."

"Your loss," she said. She stretched, bounced on her feet a little, waking her body up. "Guns?"

"Ready," said Allende, nodding to the stern of the boat where the guns rested, assembled and loaded, in their opened crate. She realized the boat was wobbling, the forward movement gone.

"Why aren't we moving?"

"We're about to raise the platform over the horizon," he said. "Wanted to make sure you had us all squared away."

"Kill the lights and let's go," she said.

DAY 8

In the darkness, they could only see the platform's lights. The top of the tower appeared first, a single red light blinking, and then more and more appeared as they murmured toward the horizon. The moon was thin, a narrow crescent in the sky, the lights of the city of Heinlein crawling across its dark face. Reina couldn't remember the last time she'd seen so many stars.

"There are people who live their whole goddamn lives and never see the stars," said Allende. "I'd never seen them until I went up-Stalk. They look so different up there. No twinkle."

"It's different in space," she said. "Blacker, somehow, even though there are even more stars, more visible."

"I heard a story that we used to believe stars were the souls of the dead. People died and went up into the heavens to be a star."

"Do you see ten million new stars up there?" she asked.

"No."

"Then I guess that old story's bullshit."

The platform grew larger and larger. She checked her Specter and found it still in place. She pulled out both LAAVs from the other crate. She launched one, tucked the other into a satchel with some other tools, and then slung it over her shoulder. The drone hummed away.

More lights appeared, a string of flashing red along the high towers, and then the livable levels appeared, lit with a warm orange glow and the occasional floodlight. She called up a virt display from her skinsuit for Allende's benefit to show what her recon drone was seeing.

The platform was over a hundred meters tall, but most of it was carbosteel-lattice towers and pylons, studded with comms masts and signal lights and other machinery Reina couldn't identify. The center was dominated by a single enormous shaft that ran down beneath the waves and bulked up in the middle of the platform like a mountain. Reina recalled that the platform was used for drilling and imagined a gigantic drill bit, but that seemed unlikely. About thirty meters above the waves clustered the habitable levels: an irregular rectangle of walkways and platforms and pressure-sealed chambers, with an open-air main platform flanked by two low blockhouses. The main platform had a round landing pad suspended over the side.

"Is that a tiltjet sitting on that pad?" Allende asked. "Is it…it looks armed."

"I think Mr. Stone is here," she said. "The man who killed Rafe."

"That's good, right?"

"Maybe," she said. "We're here to extract a whistle-blower named Hector Gajula."

"But if Mr. Stone is already here, maybe he knows about Gajula," said Allende.

"Yes."

"Do we abort?"

"No," she said. "Even if we don't get Gajula or his data, we can still take Mr. Stone off the board."

"You are a scary lady." The LAAV continued to circle the platform, then zoomed in on a pair of men walking along the edge of the main level. They were both wearing dark fatigues with armored vests and carrying small-caliber submachine guns. "Is that a normal amount of security for a facility like this one?" asked Allende.

"I don't know," she said. "I don't think so. Physical security should be light—the hard part is even getting out here."

As they watched, a door opened and a woman emerged. She was wearing civilian dress, brown shorts and a light jacket against the night breeze. Reina pegged her as a tech or researcher, someone low ranked. The sec team stopped her and they talked briefly. One secman gestured with his gun. The woman went back inside.

"I don't understand what just happened," she said.

"She looked scared," said Allende. "Frag. These guys aren't security. I think they're jailers."

"Keeping the staff locked down while he tries to plug the leak," she said. "He doesn't know it's Gajula, just that it's someone on the platform."

"What does he do if he can't figure out who it is?"

She shrugged. "Kills them all and throws them into the ocean, I imagine," she said.

Allende swore.

As they came into the shadow of the platform she re-tasked the LAAV. Laser communications required line of sight, and they were passing under the platform itself. She maneuvered the recon drone into position to catch the Specter's signal and repeat it down to the *Princess Rosie*. The connection to the laser comms array on the *Rosie* would itself be wireless somewhere in the radio spectrum, and detectable, but Reina was more concerned with eavesdropping on Grendel's outgoing messages than the secrecy of her own comms. As long as her secretary was in charge of the security systems, her comms were invisible anyway.

Once under the platform, the sound changed. The roar of the ocean echoed and crashed in the carbosteel-lattice above them, coming back and around into a complex texture that became part of the background. They had to raise their voices to be heard while Reina prepared the semtex charges.

"Go to each pylon in turn," Reina shouted. She scrambled onto the boat's bow. Allende slowly made his way clockwise around the outer edge of the platform, giving Reina time to leap to each pylon, plant two charges on the thick beams, and jump back to the boat. "Okay," she said. "Take us in."

"I'm making for that one there," Allende called, pointing at the thicker pylon in the center, where the main shaft descended. "It looks set up to receive boats. Get the rope ready!"

Like the sound, the waves here were crashing back and forth in every direction, and the *Rosie* bucked and grumbled, her engine growling. The engine roared as Allende backed water and the boat swung in. Reina threw out the rubber bumpers on the bow and leapt over to the pylon itself. She tied the boat on. Allende did the same at the stern, then climbed up, *tsked* at her knot, and retied the boat.

Reina jumped down and handed up the guns one by one. She paused and attached silencers to the pistols, then tossed a satchel full of extra magazines up onto the pylon's flat concrete deck. Allende slung the satchel over his shoulder. Reina dug through it and transferred a few of the magazines within to her own bag. She took her gun back from Allende and wore that over her shoulder. The pistol she touched to her leg and her skinsuit grabbed it, holding it fast. Allende jammed his into the waistband of his shorts.

They made their way across the algae-smeared concrete to a ladder of heavy steel rungs. Reina could see it comfortably with her cyber-enhanced eyes, but Allende seemed to be navigating mostly by feel in the darkness. "They must have an elevator," said Allende. "On one of these pylons, at least."

"Want to turn on a floodlight and look for it?"

"No," he grimaced. "Okay, you first." She climbed. At first she tried to do it without using any of her suit's power, but she found her arm still weak. Grudgingly, she let the suit assist her. When she was almost at the top she paused and looked down. Allende was only a quarter of the way up, blowing hard. She went back down and took his satchel and his rifle. His legs snarled with each rung, and he didn't have enough wind to spare to thank her. She climbed back to the top and came carefully up through the hole in the deck.

The ladder emptied into a little alcove between a metal-lattice tower and a blockhouse with long windows overlooking the central area of the platform. She saw no sign of the sec team, so she set Allende's gun and satchel down and pulled out the second LAAV. She sent it up and set it to patrol the top level, then used her admin rights on the platform security system to skim through camera feeds. She found the two secguards on the platform and four more scattered throughout the rest of the facility. She didn't find Mr. Stone or Gajula, which worried her.

She waited for Allende, standing guard with her pistol in hand. By the time he came huffing and blowing up the last few rungs, the patrolling sec team had reached the center of the platform…and noticed her drone.

"What's that?" asked one, his voice caught by the recon drone's mic and relayed to Reina's senses via wireless.

"Recon drone," said the other.

"No time to catch your breath," Reina hissed. "We have to move now."

"Wait," said Allende, but she was moving. The first step was to jam wireless, sending a signal to her console to broadcast a wash of noise throughout the spectrum.

The second step was to round the corner, her handgun raised. One of the secmen was tapping at his wrist-mounted PAD, wondering why his message wasn't going through. The other raised his submachine gun and put a single bullet through the drone. The poor dumb thing had no evasion subroutines installed, and it simply squawked and fluttered to the deck.

Reina shot the secman with his finger on the trigger first, just as he spun in her direction. Enhanced senses, or glasses-mounted compressed 360? She didn't know and it didn't matter. Her gun coughed and her bullet took him in the center of his face and he crumpled backward like a doll. His friend was turning as well, already firing wildly, bullets spanging and sparking on the metal of the rig to her right. She adjusted her aim as he dropped into a crouch, and her first shot plucked at his shoulder, sending the fabric of his uniform belling out like a child's fingers had touched him. He staggered and she shot him twice more, once in the chest, where her bullet was stopped by his breastplate, and again in the head, sending a spray of red across the platform. He fell.

Allende came around with his assault rifle in ready position. He walked a slow circle, his legs whirring. "Two down. I don't see anyone else."

Reina checked the camera footage, flickering it across her vision. "No, we're alone up here. But there are four more secguards and they heard that gunfire." She retrieved her rifle. "They're moving. Wait. I just lost two of them."

"Lost them?"

"There must be a room in the facility with no cameras. That's why I can't find Mr. Stone. He's in there."

Allende spat. "No cameras. Wonder what he's doing in there." Allende led the way toward the closest doors while Reina came half-focused along behind him, splitting attention between the cameras and her own body. "Can you find the hidden room? Figure out where it is by tracking what you can see?"

"Yes," she said, "but it will take time. Two of the secguards have just realized their friends aren't answering their calls and they're putting on their helmets and more armor."

"Who else is here?"

"About a dozen civilian staff." She panned through the cameras quickly, finding nervous-looking people sitting on beds in dormitories, whispering together in what looked like a cafeteria, a handful still sleeping. "Wait."

On the vid, the cafeteria doors opened and the two armored secmen stepped through. One of the civilians, the woman with the brown shorts from before, stepped forward to ask them something.

The secmen lifted their submachine guns and sent a cluster of bullets through the center of her chest. From the angle of the camera, Reina watched a red ragged hole erupt in the back of her jacket. The woman fell and the other four civilians in the room screamed, scrambling to their feet. The secmen kept firing, methodically, with no wasted movements. They murdered everyone.

"They're killing the civilians," Reina said.

"Where?" said Allende. "For god's sake, where?"

"Cafeteria and dorms, lower level, that building." She pointed. Allende took off at a run, his legs complaining. Reina jogged after, unlimbering her rifle and touching the handgun back to her leg. "Corporal, this isn't the mission!"

"Like hell," he said. The door didn't open at his approach, but the security recognized Reina and it hissed wide while he was scrambling for an override. He rushed through. The foyer had doors across and corridors to the left and right, and a staircase down. He went down to another set of secure doors. Again they hissed open as Reina approached.

Beyond was a corridor running to the right and ahead. "Which way?" Allende asked, and then a crack of gunfire sounded from ahead. He didn't wait for her answer.

The cameras went dead, suddenly. All of them, at the same

time. "I'm blind," Reina said. "They might be able to see us now."

Allende shoved through a heavy swinging door. They passed the cafeteria on the right. Reina didn't look inside.

They entered a locker room where rows of tall metal cabinets divided the space into a labyrinth. A heavy, metal hatch stood open to the sea air beyond, and the hiss of water to the right suggested showers, but Reina couldn't see them.

Allende crossed the room to the hatch. "There's someone out here. I think he's still alive."

Reina stalked forward, listening. She wished she'd brought thermal optics, or that her eyes had been upgraded to include thermal imaging. With her connection to the platform's cams cut off and her recon drone shot down, she felt blind.

Allende stepped through the hatch. A small sphere clanked from between the rows of lockers to roll about on the floor.

"Grenade!" Reina stepped back, turning herself away from the blast. Allende dropped and the sphere burst with an intense, bright, burning light. Reina's eyes cut out, shutting themselves off deliberately to prevent permanent damage. Her ears had no such protection and exploded with high-pitched ringing.

Her vision came back quickly and she ducked to her left, tucking herself into the cover of a bank of lockers just as a thunder of bullets punched through the air where she had crouched. She saw Allende stumble and stagger, dropping to his knees. He scrambled back into the locker room as the hatch whirred shut, crushing into his legs behind him. He sprawled, and she saw him struggling to rise. His legs were trapped.

Reina moved again, back to the hallway door, her rifle up. Allende fumbled with his gun, but it was no use—he couldn't get an angle on the room from where he lay. Reina saw a shadow of movement, the secmen working forward to get a line of sight on Allende. She trained her weapon and fired twice. The movement stopped.

They couldn't see her, she realized. Her console's jamming was still up, preventing them from receiving wireless data from the building security. Whoever was sitting on command could see her, but these two couldn't. She moved again, ducking to the next row of lockers on her right, and barely got there before another cluster of bullets tore through the air over her shoulder. Her hearing was slowly returning—she could hear Allende swearing as he struggled.

She darted from locker to locker, trying to get a bead on the secman stalking her. Twice she thought she had him and fired, but he'd shifted position and she had to dive to avoid a spray of small-caliber bullets. She doubled back, and then the secman stepped into view, blocking her retreat.

The moment crystallized as she realized she was dead, raising her rifle and knowing that she was too slow.

The secman's face was hidden behind his visor, but it left his mouth clear and she watched him grin and somehow that was the worst part.

She heard the crack of a rifle and then the secman's head burst as an explosive shell went off inside his helmet.

She turned and saw Allende sitting on the floor not far from the hatch. His legs ended in stumps with metal caps above the knee; he had simply detached his trapped legs and shuffled himself into position. He gave her a thumbs-up and panned his rifle across the room, looking for threats through the scope. She crouched down herself and raised the Neo Muscovite rifle, overlaying its targeting suite on her vision through the skinsuit's connection at the stock. A targeting reticle appeared in her vision.

"Nothing on thermal," Allende called. "Could they have thermal damping on that armor?" He shuffled forward, using his hands to slide across the deck.

"No," she said. "The showers," and turned, but it was too late, and the second secman shot Allende in the chest and throat and head with a short *pop-pop-pop* burst. He was crouch-walking out of the showers, where his thermal signature had been hidden, his armor still wet, and Reina put the targeting reticle right over his heart as the barrel of his gun spun toward her.

He was wearing carapace armor, but her ammo had been selected with carapace armor in mind. The first round hit at an angle and deflected off the hard plating, but the next two punched right through, deforming and blooming as they went, and turned his rib cage into a red soup. There was no way he was getting up again.

The pain in her arm was so brutal that it flared and died, her mods switching the nerves off to keep her from going into shock. She realized she was lying on the deck and that she had been shot, the secman having squeezing off a burst when her first bullet deflected. She struggled to sit. The secman was dying, noisily, and she fumbled for the pistol at her side, found it, and shot him until he finally stopped moving.

Her left arm hung limp at her side. A pool of blood shone on the deck beneath her, smearing and growing. Not as much as it could be; her skinsuit was putting pressure on her arm, cutting off the blood. She didn't probe the wound.

Standing proved harder than she thought; she felt lightheaded. She staggered to Allende's side. He was dead.

"Soldiers die in war," she said. She crouched down and closed his eyes. She wondered if she should say something else. Instead, she took his gun and slung it over her shoulder. "Kick ass as hard as I can, any way that I can," she said. The gun was heavy. She carried it anyway, hauling herself into the cafeteria. Along the way, she located and shot out the cameras.

When she reached the cafeteria, she laid her arsenal across the surface of a table, sat, and laboriously reloaded each gun. The work went slowly with only one hand. She kept one eye on the entrances, on the glassed-over bay windows out into the corridors. The enemy wouldn't be able to approach without her noticing.

The enemy didn't approach. She fashioned a sling for her arm, threw the assault rifle over her shoulder, and used her dead left arm to brace the Neo Muscovite semi-auto. It was as close as she was likely to get to combat ready. She took a stim. It helped.

She had a schematic of the platform, but it wasn't labeled. She found what she assumed was security control by studying the wiring, looking for where the majority of the data lines centered.

She also found what must have been GRNDL's main laboratories. For a moment, she hesitated. Gajula was the mission. Extracting him alive was already impossible—Mr. Stone had certainly ordered him, along with every other civilian aboard the platform, killed. His data was the next best thing. Would it be on the platform's servers? Or on a memory diamond located somewhere else on the platform? Was Gajula wired, like Perrault or Reina herself?

She didn't know. She headed for the labs, down into the guts of the platform. She found a tall, echoing chamber with a massive cylindrical piston running through its heart. Part of the platform's drilling apparatus, she assumed—some sort of geothermal power technology. Was it as simple as drilling too deeply, triggering an earthquake? Gajula's data would have the answer.

The labs overlooked the central chamber. She could see the tall stacks of parallel quantum rigs humming through the bay windows. She climbed a rickety steel staircase, not daring to release her rifle to steady herself on the handrail. It was harder than it should have been.

When she reached the lab she studied the systems. All were linked, presumably to workstations throughout the complex or wirelessly to individual researchers' PADs. She regretted for a moment not lifting a PAD off one of the corpses in the living area—it would have made it easier. She ran a line from her console to one of the hard ports on the server cluster and was immediately confronted with a wall of ice.

She looked around. No sign of the enemy. "Frag it." She jacked in.

Her body fell away. She was underwater, swimming, drowning, and then she broke through and was hanging in her ready space. She called up the chessboard and attacked, furiously, almost blindly. As in her initial run via the drone, she found the server only lightly protected. The white pieces were quickly surrounded and eliminated by her knights and rooks, and her pawns advanced unimpeded. She was in. She unleashed her crawlers and found nothing. Gajula's data wasn't here. She jacked out.

When she returned to her body, she was staring into the barrel of a gun. "Sorry, lady," the secwoman holding it said. "You had a good run, but—"

Reina grabbed the gun and twisted, boosting her strength, tearing it out of the woman's hand. She stood, looming, and lashed out, swinging the gun into the woman's temple. Her visor spiderwebbed and the woman lurched back.

"Jesus!" Another voice, behind her, and Reina turned and then everything went white and confused. "Zi, you okay?"

She was on her knees. Her hands were being cuffed behind her. She could see the secwoman, tearing her helmet off. "I'm bleeding. She hits like a truck. Not even human." She spat blood, glared death at Reina.

"Boss wants her alive." The voice behind her was male.

"Not forever he doesn't." Zi stood and retrieved her gun. "Take her weapons. Let's get her down to Control."

Control was a bay of virt monitors showing camera feeds from throughout the complex. She saw the *Rosie* bobbing on the water—it was still tied to the massive central pylon. She saw corpses scattered through the complex in places she hadn't shot out the cameras.

Zi and her partner marched Reina through Control and into a small, dark back room with two chairs. Mr. Stone stood from one, making room for her. Gajula, or his corpse, slumped in the other.

"Ms. Zi, Mr. Renard, thank you. Cuff her to the chair, please." They cuffed her to the chair. Mr. Stone stood before her, pulling on a fresh set of blue plastic gloves. She saw that a PX-series bioroid stood inert in one corner—Davy. "Check her feet," said Mr. Stone as he slipped in small earbuds, and Zi and Renard crouched down in front of her.

Mr. Stone drew an Argus-made hand cannon, the sort of enormous revolver that ought to be obsolete but still spat death as effectively as nearly any modern weapon, and shot Zi and Renard through their heads with a pair of deafening cracks.

Mr. Stone said a few more things she couldn't hear, and Davy came to life, dragged the corpses out of the room, then went back to his corner and switched off. Her hearing slowly returned while Mr. Stone removed his earbuds. He kept the gloves. He pulled her console off her back, examined it casually, and smashed it to pieces with the butt of his gun.

"You have to switch the bioroid off while you work," she said. "But eventually they must figure out what you do, and the First Directive must kick in."

"Yes," he said. "Then I wipe their memory or just kill them."

"Like you killed Zi and Renard?"

"No witnesses means no witnesses," he said. "I hope you're not complaining. You killed four of their associates not half an hour ago."

"That's different," she said.

"Is it?" he asked. "We're not as different as you think." He paced, clasping his hands behind his back, still holding the gun. One finger tapped against the trigger guard. His suit shimmered as he moved.

"Why am I still alive?" she asked.

"I need to ask you some questions," he said. "I don't think you'll be surprised by any of them." He turned to face her. "What's your name?"

"La Reina Roja."

"You know how rare it is I ask that question, Reina?" He resumed pacing, not waiting for an answer. "I always know everything about my subjects before we even meet. Not you, though. You don't exist. That tells me a lot about you all on its own."

"Does my name matter?" she asked.

"No," he said. "I know you were EWS, both from your skills in electronic intrusion and from the skinsuit you're still wearing. The hair is a nice touch, by the way, draws the eye away from the face. Way I figure, you're either Celeste Jimenez, who was killed in action, or maybe Mariposa, no last name given, who a few of my contacts remember getting busted for an inappropriate relationship with an enlisted man, but whose records are conveniently missing." He turned back. "I'm leaning toward the second. You didn't start being a pain in the ass until after that same enlisted man died."

She said nothing.

"I wanted you to know that, no matter how good you think you are at hiding your past, I can find it." He crouched down in front of her. "I can find it. Which means I can find your family. You're a strong, brave woman. I'm not going to torture you. What would be the point? But I can make you this promise. You play straight with me, you answer my questions, and your family stays out of it. I won't have any reason to go after them."

"Alright," she said. "Ask your questions." She tested her wireless connection. It was, miraculously, still live. Her console was dead, the jamming with it, but Mr. Stone must have figured that it was her only connection to the Network. He didn't know her skinsuit was a passable PAD in its own right.

"How much does Perrault know about this?"

"Only that Gajula was going to turn whistle-blower," Reina said. "It looks like you solved that problem."

Mr. Stone turned to glance at Gajula, as if he'd forgotten that he was there. "So it was Gajula. I thought so."

"You killed him and you didn't even know he was the mole?"

"Oh, is this the part where you call me a murderer and judge me and go off on your idealistic screed?" He turned back. He smiled. It did not make him look friendlier. "This coming from a monster."

"I'm not a monster. I'm as human as you are."

"On that we agree." He walked over to Gajula, nudging the corpse with the barrel of his gun. Reina sent a command down to *Rosie*. She had to send it twice; at this range, with this much metal in between them, the connection was spotty. She wished she were still using her console's more powerful transmitter, not her skin-suit's emergency backup. "Not the first time you've been called a monster, I bet."

"We all got mods in the War."

"True," he said. "I know I did. What, you didn't know? We're both soldiers, Maria. Reina. Whatever. Told you, we're not as different as you think."

"I'm a servicewoman. You're a murderer."

"Maybe. But we're both monsters. And it's not for the reason you think. Respirocytes in the blood, boosted metabolism, enhanced strength—these aren't the things that make us monsters, that make us inhuman." He waved the gun. "It's not what we are. It's what we do. We kill. Without remorse, without hesitation."

"I only kill the enemy."

"And who defines 'enemy'? I kill when I have orders. When I have a mission that requires it. You're the same way, except you don't have a superior officer giving you direction. You're just some sad, desperate madwoman murdering your way across New Angeles."

Pings came in from both drones. They were in range. She dropped the pilot program for the Specter into her skinsuit's memory and took stock. "Weren't you asking questions?"

"Who else knows you came here?"

"No one," she said. "Perrault told me where to find Gajula, but I didn't run my op by her before I launched." She quickly hit a closed door. She hopped over to the LAAV and sent it crashing into the latch. The door opened. The Specter slipped through.

"Were you the source of CEL's data? Did you feed that file to Rafe Cruz?"

"Yes."

"Where did you get it?"

"Off a server in the NA Gateway Stacks. Blind chance; I was

chasing after GPI records to expose that they'd lied to the military during the War."

"No one inside GRNDL or GPI told you where to look?" He folded his arms, the gun dangling casually from one hand.

The Specter's autonav was up to the task of getting to Control. She jacked out and focused on her hands. She was cuffed, not bound in plastic—probably Mr. Stone had figured that she could break the plastic ties and opted for a stronger chain to bind her. She might be able to break this one, too, but not without him noticing. Mr. Stone would simply shoot her dead. "No, no one told me where to look. I've been chasing data intercepts and sniffing packets for months."

"Six nights ago," he said. "You pulled data from a GRNDL server in Amazonas." The nerves from her left arm were already dead. She sent some instructions to her skinsuit, which broke her thumb and folded her hand down to slip through the cuff. She didn't feel it. "What did you get? Where is that data now?" He wandered to the doorway, peering out into Control. Frantic, she jacked back in and grabbed control of the Specter, holding its position just outside the control room.

"I was only able to download a file fragment," she said. "I was never able to salvage anything from it. You just smashed my only remaining copy."

"Thank you," he said, coming back into the room and studying his gun. "You've been very cooperative."

"Do you want to ask 'why' or tell me that I'm part of a dying old world to be swept aside by the new or anything?" She piloted the Specter into the control room. "That soldiers and patriots like me are deluded remnants of a world in which states were more powerful than corporations?"

"I hadn't planned on it," he said. "I mean, we can do that bit if you want, but my heart wouldn't be in it." He studied his gun for a moment. "Calling yourself a 'soldier' is a bit of a stretch though, don't you think? You're more of a talented amateur when it comes to the craft. I suppose EWS didn't train you to handle a rifle, not really."

The Specter floated through the door. Its AI flagged her as friendly and Mr. Stone as hostile and requested kill authority.

"No, they trained me as a drone operator." Reina gave the authorization.

The Specter coughed and deployed one of its three flechette rounds, hurling an expanding cluster of razor-sharp blades at Mr. Stone at just under the speed of sound.

Mr. Stone spun, maybe warned by the tone of her voice, maybe by his glasses' heads-up display, and the flechettes missed his torso, shredding his right shoulder and upper arm. His gun slipped through pain-deadened fingers, clattering over the deck, and Reina pulled herself free from the chair. She rushed to Gajula, tore open his shirt, and boosted power to her fingers. Behind her, she heard the Specter cough again and Mr. Stone moving. There was a hatch in the floor, she noticed, behind Gajula. Mr. Stone vanished through it, pulling it shut behind him.

She tore into Gajula's flesh with her fingers and found the memory diamond implanted in his sternum. She pulled it free, trailing its tiny lacework wiring like roots. She stood. She wobbled.

"Davy, wake up," she said. The bioroid in the corner woke up and stepped toward her. "I'm bleeding badly and about to pass out, and the platform is going to explode. You have to take me to the airplane on the main level and fly me back to the mainland."

"Where is the boss?" asked Davy.

"He'll be fine," Reina said.

"Why is the platform going to explode?" The bioroid came closer as she wobbled.

"Because someone put semtex charges along every pylon foot and they're about to go off."

"We must save as many people as we can," Davy said.

"Everyone else is dead," she said, and took him into the control room and showed him.

"Ah," said Davy. "Who killed all these people?"

"Your boss, mostly," she said. "'No witnesses means no witnesses.' Now take me to the plane and get me out of here."

She set off the charges as the tiltjet lifted off. She guessed that Mr. Stone had had about three minutes to make it off the platform. He might have survived. She'd find out later.

She blacked out.

Day 42

I'm sorry, sir, but those funds are currently locked." The secretary's voice buzzed over the virt, too cheap and dumb to even bother with a convincing human tone.

"Unlock them, then, you son of a silicon—!" Morris took a deep breath. Getting angry at an AI never solved anything.

"The funds will remain locked until the grand jury investigation ends, Mr. Morris. Thank you for banking with Titan Transnational. Good day." The virt flared and died and the secretary vanished.

Morris swore again and threw the PAD against the wall. He screamed; he clenched his fists. He grabbed one of the chairs and threw it over the stone balustrade into the tangle of green below. He needed a drink. "Wanda!" he shouted. "Get me a whiskey."

He took a deep breath, trying to calm down. So he couldn't get at his money until the grand jury was convinced he hadn't broken any laws to earn that money. No big deal. He'd bought the house at a good rate after being evicted from Paradise Arcology; he could afford it. If things got really bad, he could dip into his offworld accounts in the Martian money haven Locke had hooked him up with, even though he wasn't supposed to touch it so the lawyers didn't find it, so his hag of a wife didn't steal it in all in the divorce, because she'd left him when everything collapsed, ungrateful…

His breathing sped up. His knuckles whitened.

He really needed a drink.

He turned his back on the darkening Andes and muttered his way into the house. "Wanda!" he shouted. "Where's that whiskey?" He passed into the living room. The wall lit up with a newsfeed and stock ticker—GRNDL was down again—and he watched while he tore at his tie. It was about the quake. A scientist-looking Asian guy was talking to that sexy nosie, Lockwell.

"The New Angeles tsunami was caused by the massive displacement of water after a megathrust quake on the Nazca fault line, not far from the New Angelino coast. Such earthquakes have happened before at multiple points in Ecuador's history. The GRNDL platform did experience its own—much smaller—earthquake, yes, but it was over seven hundred kilometers away. Based on the evidence, I would argue that GRNDL did not cause the tsunami."

"Thank you," said Morris. "Finally, someone talking a lick of sense."

"What about the so-called 'earthquake cascade'? Isn't it possible that the fault-line quake was triggered by smaller earthquakes that were themselves caused by the GRNDL platform?" Morris threw his tie at the screen. He wondered why he'd ever thought that bitch journo was pretty.

"Screen off," he said. The screen didn't turn off. "Screen off!"

"That's just a theory, one not well supported by the facts. No one has yet managed to use the model to predict a future earthquake."

"Except for the fact that GRNDL seismologists predicted the New Angeles quake, and had their prediction not just ignored by GRNDL, but silenced by that same corporation. And we still don't know why that platform sank."

"Ms. Lockwell, I have no idea where you're coming from with these accusations. I'm not on GRNDL's payroll, and I'm telling you that the evidence doesn't indicate that the tsunami was induced by human activity."

"Not on GRNDL's payroll," said Lockwell, and her grin was like a wolf taking off its sheep costume. "But all your research for the last five years has been funded by the Blue Sky Council, which is a

Weyland Consortium research think tank. I think that's a connection that our viewers deserve to know."

The screen froze on the scientist's fishlike gape, and Morris turned away in disgust. He saw Wanda's silhouette standing over the couch. "Wanda," he said. "Get me that whiskey, then figure out what's wrong with the wall. Call an expert if you have to."

He undid his cuffs, waiting for her response. She didn't move. She didn't say anything. She was switched off. "Wanda, wake up." She didn't wake up. The wall blinked off. Suddenly, he was afraid and alone in the dark.

He heard a movement behind him and turned to shout but the darkness burst into a flare of bright red pain. He was on his knees, blood dripping from his mouth, and a tall, broad-shouldered woman was standing over him with a gun pressed against his forehead.

"John Morris," she said, and it wasn't a question.

"Yes," he said. "I can pay you, I swear to god—"

"With what money? Your offworld Martian accounts? I already have them."

"No," he said, "no, Locke said it was untraceable—"

"You care more about money than human lives," she said. "Even your own."

"Now, wait," he said.

"Did you give the order to kill Rafe Cruz?"

"Who? I don't even know who that is!"

"Did you order the Grendel platform staff to continue drilling, even after being warned by Hector Gajula and others of the danger?"

"You don't understand," he said, "I had my own problems. I only had eighteen months to prove viability of the project, or Weyland would pull funding and I'd never work again!"

"Who did you share the Gajula report with? Who were your bosses at Weyland?" He hesitated, and she jammed the gun against him, knocking him back.

"The board! I don't know the names of everyone on the board, they're...the board!" She cocked the gun. "I...I...Elizabeth Mills! Mills is on the board of directors, she made me her pet project, she told me to continue, god, I didn't want to, I mean, think of the disaster if something did happen, right? And I was right!

Something did happen and it ruined us! GRNDL is a shell now, an empty corp with no assets. It could take years to recover!"

"You are the enemy," she said. "You are everything that I am at war with. Your greed and selfish fear killed millions of innocents."

"Only thousands!" He felt her stiffen, realized it was the wrong tack. "It wasn't me," he said, scrambling backward. He was looking for something, anything, he could find—an ashtray, a vase, a PAD, something to bash this madwoman's head in with. "Don't you get it? Killing me won't do any good: it won't give you any satisfaction."

"No," she said. "It's a small victory. But the War continues." She shot him three times in the chest and head.

About the Author

Daniel Lovat Clark is a professional nerd and cocreator of the *Android* setting. He works as a writer and game developer at Fantasy Flight Games, where his credits include work on *Android: Netrunner, Descent: Journeys in the Dark, Warhammer Fantasy Roleplay,* and several *Star Wars* roleplaying games.

He lives in the Twin Cities with a dog, a daughter, two cats, and a wife who may technically qualify as the third cat.

IT IS THE FUTURE. THE WORLD CHANGED. PEOPLE DID NOT.

Humanity has spread itself across the solar system with varying degrees of success. The Moon and Mars are colonized. A plan to terraform the Red Planet is well underway, hindered only by a civil war that has broken out and locked down many of its habitation domes. On Earth, a massive space elevator has been built near the equator in the sprawling megapolis of New Angeles, stretching up into orbit. Known colloquially as "the Beanstalk," it is the hub of trade between the worlds, especially for the helium-3 that powers fusion reactors and the modern economy.

Discoveries in computing and neurobiology now allow a human mind to be stored electronically in braintapes and then emulated to create strong artificial intelligence. The same research also has given rise to sophisticated brain-machine interfaces that allow users to feed data into their neurons and experience the Network in a whole new way. Advances in genetics and cybernetics allow people to modify or augment themselves at will, pushing the boundaries of what it means to be human.

Enormous megacorporations, called "corps" by most, influence every facet of daily life: food, threedee, music, career choices. Jinteki and Haas-Bioroid redefine life itself, making clones and bioroids with artificial brains using the latest neural conditioning and neural channeling techniques. The Weyland Consortium owns a piece of everything that goes up or down the Beanstalk—and everything goes up or down the Beanstalk. And NBN shapes what the masses think and dream, with the most extensive media network ever conceived on Earth under its control.

Despite the technological advances, human nature remains as complex and dark as ever. The men, women, and androids of the New Angeles Police Department struggle to keep order in the largest city in human history, while hundreds of murders are committed every day. Human First, a violent anti-android hate group, stages protests and uses heavy sledgehammers to destroy the "golems," the androids they blame for all society's ills. Crime is rampant, with orgcrime outfits deeply penetrated into law enforcement, politics, and the megacorps. Illegal Netcriminals called "runners" use the Network to enrich themselves, oppose corporate hegemony, and experiment with new technology.

EARLY REVERSION ACTIVISTS

As the end of the century approaches, so does the end of the groundbreaking Quito Accord. Unfortunately, what was supposed to be a smooth and peaceful transition of power has become fraught with social and political strife. For a number of reasons—bad faith on the part of the U.S. government, loopholes in the wording of the treaty—activist groups have sprung up calling for an early end to the Accord. These so-called early reversion activist groups (ERAs) range from relatively peaceful, grass-roots community organizations to staid political action groups to bomb-throwing radicals. While dozens are active in New Angeles, three groups' actions have attracted the New Angeles Police Department's notice: Consejo por un Ecuador Libre, La Brigada Tricolor, and the Pan-American Council.

CONSEJO POR UN ECUADOR LIBRE

Consejo por un Ecuador Libre (CEL), or, the Council for a Free Ecuador, is a small, grass-roots organization based in the Antiguo Guayaquil District of New Angeles. The CEL was founded less than a decade ago by a group of longtime Guayaquil residents led by Professor Atoc Amador and anti-colonialism activist Beatriz Velasco. Dedicated to a free, Ecuadorian New Angeles, they are at once the loudest and the weakest politically of the top three ERA groups on the NAPD's watch list. Formed in the wake of a bloody NAPD crackdown on a large anti-colonialism protest, the group is largely composed of street-level activists, community organizers, and several local fringe politicians. Most of these people are the descendants of native Ecuadorians who, when the Quito Accord was signed and the area became American territory, became aliens in their own land.

Despite the organization's youth and relative political impotence, the CEL has become a mainstream activist group among native Ecuadorians living in New Angeles. By combining their early reversion issues with anti-poverty, pro-labor, and anti-corporate agitation, they appeal to a broad section of Ecuadorians. Unfortunately, their impoverished state limits the scope and effectiveness of their tactics, and they are reduced to spreading their message via word-of-mouth and passing out actual dead-tree paper leaflets on street corners.

The CEL calls for an early end to the Quito Accord and a reversion of New Angeles to Ecuadorian control. They claim that the United States has violated both the terms and the spirit of the Accord, and that due to this, Ecuador can claim legal sovereignty over New Angeles. To assist them in their cause, the CEL has allied with a number of social justice advocacy groups throughout New Angeles. They believe that this alliance of pro-labor, anti-corp, anti-government, and anti-colonialism groups will make the CEL more powerful and harder to ignore, especially in the face of opposition from establishment forces. Whether this unified front will help these activists make their point remains to be seen, however.

Although passionate about their cause, CEL's supporters suffer from an overabundance of optimism, enthusiasm, and belief in the better nature humanity. While certainly laudable, this enthusiasm lends itself to a certain wide-eyed political naiveté that is both charming and infuriating, especially for their allies. In addition, they are a fractious, polarized group much given to infighting, disagreements about ideological purity, and endless meetings at which little gets accomplished. These factors, combined with their stunted treasury and street-level tactics, make them both easily dismissed and easily manipulated by their opponents.

LA BRIGADA TRICOLOR

The majority of ERA groups operating in New Angeles espouse legal, non-violent means to their ends. There are some, however, who support a more aggressive, bloodier agenda. The chief among these groups is a small but extremely dangerous organization known as La Brigada Tricolor.

Taking its name from the Ecuadorian flag, La Brigada is a dangerous group of fanatics who hide their insidious goals behind a facade of populism and Ecuadorian nationalism. At its core, La Brigada is a violent terrorist group bent on seizing control of New Angeles for their own ends. Led by a shadowy figure known only as "El Jefe," La Brigada supports not only an early end to the Quito Accord but also New Angeles' secession from both Ecuador and the United States. Its end game—at least,

its publicly stated end game—is an autonomous Nuevo Angeles Libre operating as a city-state with its own governmental and military apparatus free from outside interference.

Among La Brigada's leadership however, the end game is seen differently. Rumors say that El Jefe, who the NAPD believes is a highly placed member of the Los Scorpiones orgcrime syndicate, has other plans—plans that have little to do with freedom or high ideals. Where other activist groups are, ostensibly, working for the betterment of New Angelinos and either New Angeles or Ecuador as a whole, La Brigada is only interested in gaining power and wealth for themselves. To this end, it has undertaken a campaign of terrorism against both governmental and civilian targets. La Brigada agents have attacked every region of the city in their mission to destabilize and delegitimize the sitting government. They were allegedly behind the

bombings of the NAPD Headquarters building as well as the Root. They are also believed to be responsible for the riot that burned the undercity levels of Haas-Bioroid's Milaflores Arcology in the Manta District. They have also claimed responsibility for the infamous NBN Angel Arena broadcast interruption and a massive, well-coordinated denial of service attack that brought much of the city's network infrastructure to its knees for more than six hours, although NBN's own records indicate this outage never occurred.

After every attack, El Jefe releases another combination press release/manifesto taking responsibility for the attacks and calling for a free New Angeles. While this approach has garnered the group a number of powerful enemies, it has also earned a

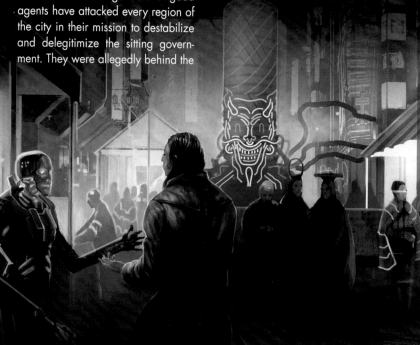

lumber of powerful allies, especially among the city's powerful organized crime syndicates and a handful of influential and corrupt politicians.

THE PAN-AMERICAN COUNCIL

The Pan-American Council (PAC) is an oddity among the many vociferous ERA groups in New Angeles. The PAC is composed largely of wealthy elites—politicians, high-ranking corporate officers, media personalities, lawyers, powerful lobbyists, and professional activists—who have a vested interest in maintaining the status quo. To that end, the PAC endorses compromise and appeasement. It calls for an extension of the terms of the Quito Accord combined with a gradual turnover of select American assets to Ecuadorian control. These elements, largely small bits of governmental apparatus and a handful of inconsequential American-held corporations, would be nationalized by Ecuador to make both countries equal partners in the administration of New Angeles. The PAC's ultimate goal is a sort of hybrid American and Ecuadorian control of the city.

Even the most casual observers fear that the PAC's solution to the end of the Quito Accord is both completely unworkable and a losing proposition for the Ecuadorian government. The suggested concessions to the Ecuadorian government would increase the burden on an already-strained government while affording Ecuador no increase in control over New Angeles' affairs. The plan, as written, is considered a boondoggle that will hold up true reversion for decades in mountains of red tape and endless legal challenges.

This is, of course, the whole point of the PAC's platform, according to its detractors. The gradual reversion/co-operational control scheme was never designed to work. Critics say it was created to maintain American control of New Angeles long after the expiration of the Quito Accord while cutting the Ecuadorian government in on the profits in exchange for maintaining the status quo. The elites get wealthier and more powerful, the poor stay poor, and no drastic changes take place that could threaten shareholders and corporate profits.

The CEL and many of its allies are pushing back against the PAC's blatant end-run around the Accord, but their efforts seem to be of little use. The power wielded by PAC members, who are either power-brokers themselves or the representatives of wealthy elites, is incredible. Even New Angeles Mayor Ignacio Wells has, through the occasional oblique off-record comment, shown support for the PAC and its plan. As an organization, the PAC has enough political and financial capital to quash even the most impassioned efforts to stop it. It holds most of the cards, and in a long drawn-out battle—as the fight over reversion promises to be—it has the luxury of simply sitting back and waiting while its weaker and louder opponents burn themselves out.

POWER UNLEASHED

The Geostrategic Research and Neo-thermal Development Laboratories (GRNDL) are one of the Weyland Consortium's many holdings in the energy sector. On paper, GRNDL's stated mission is the development of alternative energy sources with a focus on advanced energy extraction technologies, and they are an attractive investment for financiers who are willing to bet against the stability of the helium-3 market. To those who have even heard of them, GRNDL are an obscure but innovative energy exploration company employing hundreds of people around the Pacific Rim.

Watchdog groups, however, equate GRNDL with their dismissive attitude toward both the press and international environmental law. The most paranoid believe that there is something deeply wrong with GRNDL; they say that beneath the surface lurks a dark secret—a cold, fierce drive for profit and a callous disregard for human life that would draw protests from even the most grasping, criminal megacorp if their secrets were ever revealed.

HUMBLE BEGINNINGS

Founded in the early part of the century, GRNDL began as the project of a group of students and researchers at the University of the Californias Pasadena. Using a revolutionary new technique that extracted more natural gas in a safer, more efficient and cost-effective manner from deposits well beyond the reach of contemporary energy companies, the group secured venture capital and incorporated as a for-profit organization.

After GRNDL clinched their first contracts, they relocated from their small start-up office to an offshore complex in the Santa Barbara Channel. The true reasons for the reclusive move are shrouded in mystery, but some suspect that this was the first sign of something amiss at the company. Others point to the fierce competition in the energy sector as drastic new emissions regulations wreaked havoc on profits and the energy supply—GRNDL clearly needed to protect their proprietary techniques and research.

As time wore on, GRNDL diversified into wind, solar, and emerging nuclear technologies, and within ten years of their founding offered their first shares to the public. Their rise was not without complications, however.

PRIDE BEFORE A FALL

GRNDL's original CEO, an enthusiastic visionary named Paulo Tiradadies, disappeared while on a sport fishing expedition in the Californian Gulf. The aftermath of his disappearance saw the fracturing of the board of directors as they struggled to name a replacement.

For almost a year it looked as though GRNDL lacked a clear purpose, and profits dwindled. Eventually, after much backroom deal-making and an infusion of fresh blood into the leadership, GRNDL emerged from this dark period just in time to celebrate their twentieth anniversary.

Soon the corp's geothermal technologies were changing the face of the industry, and at the peak of GRNDL's rise they were lauded as the future of the energy industry—right up until the moment when fusion power was perfected and the helium-3 mines opened on the Moon. Almost overnight GRNDL's fortunes changed for the worse. Their stock price plummeted as shareholders divested themselves of what was now considered an old-economy energy company to invest in the hot new He-3 market. Investors, executives, and employees fled GRNDL like rats from a sinking ship, and by the middle of the century the company was a shell of its former self. GRNDL struggled to hold on for years. After a long and losing struggle, GRNDL were set to enter bankruptcy proceedings, but they were saved by a final-hour buyout.

GRNDL AND WEYLAND

Roughly twenty years ago the Weyland Consortium, known for playing the long game, was looking to invest in what insiders called "alternative energy." Helium-3 was big business, but the Lunar Insurrection and known issues with He-3 extraction showed that, while extremely lucrative, the helium isotope market was volatile.

Weyland's board could not, in good conscience, let the company's bottom line be threatened by scarcity or revolution, and they searched for ways to diversify their energy portfolio. It was during this time that GRNDL caught Weyland's eye.

Despite their hardships, and despite being reduced to a single office building located in a second-rate city in the American Northwest, GRNDL looked extremely promising. Somehow, the dying corp had managed to keep its rights to energy extraction technologies. Weyland investors saw that the acquisition of GRNDL could give the Consortium a way of diversifying its energy portfolio while acquiring new patents for practically pennies. Once Weyland contacted GRNDL's board, it took precious little effort to get CEO John Morris to agree to all of Weyland's offers, and after a perfunctory negotiation period, GRNDL became a part of the Weyland Consortium.

In the years following the acquisition, Weyland invested an impressive amount of capital into its new holding. Using GRNDL's records from their long-closed research and development department, Weyland was able to expand its foothold in the alternative energy sector with the lab's largely forgotten, once revolutionary combination gas-thermal extraction technology.

PROJECT VULCAN

Under Weyland's guidance, GRNDL are more powerful and profitable than they ever were on their own. Thanks to their innovative technologies, the company now provides a growing share of energy for remote Pacific and zaratan isles. Whatever their secret is, it is making GRNDL—and their Weyland Consortium masters—fantastic amounts of money.

According to those who have continued to track the company (primarily environmental watchdog groups), GRNDL is deeply corrupt and even dangerous. They believe the danger that GRNDL pose is more insidious—and more potentially destructive on a planet-wide scale—than the workaday corporate greed and malfeasance perpetrated by the Big Four. These opponents say that GRNDL's executives are perhaps the greediest, most power-hungry and amoral collection of individuals the modern business era has ever seen—the company does not care about the human cost of their many business ventures. Only the bottom line holds any weight with GRNDL's masters at Weyland, or so the story goes. But few, if any members of the public, have heard of GRNDL, much less the criticisms leveled against them.

None of this matters to GRNDL's executives. Their lawyers are powerful, their association with Weyland shields them from even the most dogged governmental interference, and their business interests are protected by the finest private security forces that money can buy. On the Shadow Net, rumors circulate that GRNDL's latest threat to the planet, something referred to simply as Project Vulcan, could destroy the environment. But until disaster strikes, Project Vulcan will remain no more than a ghost story invoked by the most radical environmentalists.

WHERE WERE THE WARNINGS?
Investigating the New Angeles Tsunami Casualties

Even without GRNDL's activity, Ecuador has had to contend with earthquakes throughout its history. Ecuadorian earthquakes have mainly included intraplate quakes, volcanic earthquake swarms, and interplate megathrust events from the Nazca–South American subduction zone that sometimes causes tsunamis. New Angeles has had a tsunami early warning system since before the founding of the city, and it has had to endure its share of seismic events and tidal waves.

The event now referred to as the New Angeles Tsunami was, according to some seismologists, an interplate megathrust event triggered in itself by a volcanic earthquake swarm traced back to a GRNDL drilling platform offshore. The early warning system failed—the cause of this failure is still under investigation.

One theory holds that the preceding earthquake swarm, which extended over nearly two weeks, generated so many false positives (tsunami warnings with no resulting tsunamis) that either a human operator disabled the system temporarily or the governing AI was "trained" to neglect earthquake warnings. Some wonder whether the extra fifteen minutes of evacuation afforded by a warning would have helped much at all.

When the wave train came ashore, it swamped parts of six districts and caused massive damage to New Angeles' coastal infrastructure. The total loss of life may never be known, but is estimated in the tens of thousands (plus thousands more androids, many of whom rushed into danger to save the lives of human beings).

Angela Hardwik and Collin Hsu
reporting for *The New Angelino*

» Subscribe to get all the updates as they happen!

FIRST MARTIAN EXPEDITIONARY BRIGADE

As the U.S. military brought the Lunar rebels to heel during the Worlds War, halfway across the solar system Mars erupted into open and bloody rebellion. Threats to American citizens and American corporate and governmental interests on Mars demanded an immediate response. The U.S. Armed Forces sprang into action by creating a combined arms expeditionary force to deal with the Martian insurgency—the First Mars Expeditionary Brigade.

The first order of business for the First Mars was to define its mission and create its order of battle. With the Lunar Insurrection spiraling into a corporate proxy war on Luna,

command of the new unit was given to Brigadier General named Alexander G. Puller, a member of the newly formed Space Expeditionary Corps (SXC). The corporations whose Martian assets had fallen leaned heavily on the Pentagon, and General Puller was given carte blanche to pick his command staff from among the best and brightest in the Air Force, the SXC, and the Electronic Warfare Service (EWS). Puller drew up a short list of men and women—all combat-decorated, veteran field officers he had worked with over the years—and with the service's blessing, they outlined the desired units, personnel, and materiel needed

for the mission to Mars. The result was a lean, efficient, and cohesive combined arms force formed in just eight weeks.

Within ten days of its formation, the First Mars Expeditionary Brigade embarked on a handful of converted U.S. Air Force heavy cargo vessels for the long ride to Mars. Over the intervening months, the rank-and-file of the First Mars were put through a grueling training regimen to prepare them for their assault on the Red Planet. SXC infantry units drilled, practiced boarding and landing operations on other ships in the small task force, and performed live fire and simulated small arms and munitions training. EWS personnel performed countless simulations, practicing everything from drone launches to network jamming to theater command and control. The logistics and support personnel drafted plans for breaching defenses, setting up and maintaining supply lines, and the operational priorities of the Bradbury Colony for when the First Mars reached its destination. All the while, General Puller and his staff worked twenty-hour days studying the battlefield and their opponents, and drawing up battle plans to cover every imaginable contingency.

When the First Mars arrived in orbit over the Red Planet and linked up with the corporate prisec forces that were to accompany them, they were, perhaps, the best-trained and best-prepared military force in history. They would need that training in the upcoming months, as the members of the First Mars faced a difficult guerrilla campaign against an entrenched enemy with intimate knowledge of the terrain in a lethal environment.

The First Mars Expeditionary Brigade was organized roughly along the lines as a United States Marine Corps expeditionary brigade. General Puller chose this formation to give the First Mars maximum flexibility—each unit was specifically picked to enhance the brigade's nature as a highly mobile, quick-strike force that could adjust quickly to changing tactical realities.

GROUND FORCES

The First Mars's ground forces comprised three diverse infantry units—SXC infantry, SXC mechanized infantry, and SXC marines. Regular SXC infantry, known colloquially as "straight-leg" infantry, made up the bulk of the Expeditionary Force. They performed the majority of the fighting, and as have foot soldiers throughout history, suffered the bulk of the casualties. Straight-leg infantry was augmented by faster, more heavily armed mechanized infantry—specially trained and equipped soldiers wearing powered combat exoskeletons. Finally, the SXC marines were tough, highly skilled, highly motivated troopers trained for ship and station boarding, planetary landing actions, and heavy, quick-strike attacks.

Many of the famous SXC ground units who fought in the Martian Colony Wars belonged to the First Mars. At the Battle of Bradbury, the First Mechanized Infantry distinguished themselves by preserving the infrastructure even if it meant sustaining heavier casualties, and after the battle, many of the unit's personnel were decorated for valor and conspicuous gallantry. The Fourth Light Infantry Battalion fought bravely in the face of an enemy willing to fight a battle of attrition to slow the SXC's advances, and the Fourth's dedicated actions helped turn the tide at the Siege of Demeter. Company C of the Twenty-First Mobile Artillery Battalion provided much-needed fire support at the Battle of Kasei Valles. Its members fought like demons with small arms and improvised weapons to protect their gun carriers and dozens of wounded SXC marines from Martian rebels equipped with hand-built powered hardsuits. Perhaps the most storied—and most infamous—of the First Mars's ground forces was the Third Platoon, B Company, Fourteenth SXC Marines.

Third Platoon, known as the Red Devils for the red trim on their armor and their fierce fighting style, was an SXC rifle platoon led by Lieutenant Nicholas Simon with an attached EWS raider unit. Even before making planetfall on Mars the men and women of Third Platoon gained a reputation as a professional, highly motivated, close-knit unit with an uncanny amount of esprit de corps. They were in the thick of the heaviest fighting of the war, and time and again they did their duty with courage and honor. Lieutenant Simon, an unusually passionate and well-educated young officer, was widely respected for his discipline and leadership, as well as his tendency to lead from the front in any battle.

After a string of successful missions and combat victories, the Third Platoon was almost wiped out during the Battle of Noctis Labyrinthus. A combination of crushing battle fatigue and bad intel led the platoon into a Martian insurgent trap at the foot of a narrow box canyon. Pinned down by captured artillery and assaulted by heavily armored insurgents, the Third Platoon fought for forty-eight hours straight while they desperately called for an extraction. By the time a dropship came for them, only a handful of Marines were left, among them a grievously wounded Lieutenant Simon, a grizzled sergeant named José Rafael Cruz, and a seconded EWS warrant officer whose name and records have been lost. After the disastrous engagement at Noctis Labyrinthus, the Third Platoon was rebuilt, but was never the same. Without Lieutenant Simon at its head, and with so many of the original members dead, the Red Devils name and patch were retired, and the unit was renamed.

AEROSPACE FORCES

Like the ground forces, the aerospace forces of the First were separated into three broad unit types—dropships, starships, and drones. Its aerospace forces were regular SXC, manned and led by SXC personnel and operating under the SXC chain of command. Their role was to provide transport, close air support, observation, and aerospace command and control to the brigade's ground forces. Their inclusion in the expeditionary force was pivotal to the brigade's mobility and striking power, and indeed, without the aerospace forces, the brigade's ground forces would have suffered greatly in versatility and combat effectiveness.

Unlike the First Mars's ground forces, who were deployed solely on the Martian surface and dealt with a single theater of operation, the aerospace forces operated in three theaters—the Martian theater, Phobos theater, and Deimos theater. In each theater, various aerospace units provided transport and close air support for ground forces and struggled against Martian forces for air superiority. They expanded on the space combat lessons learned on Luna, and developed a number of new techniques to take advantage of the thin Martian atmosphere and pock-marked surface.

As with the ground forces, the First Mars's aerospace forces distinguished themselves through their bravery and through a dashing, devil-may-care attitude that permeated every aspect of their service. The Twentieth Rescue Squadron was one of the most

Task Force One, First Mars

Perhaps the single most important element of the First Mars's aerospace forces was the task force of heavy starships that transported the brigade from Earth to Mars. A motley selection of varied ship classes, nearly all of the heavies that were pressed into service to haul the First Mars across the system started their lives as commercial cargo haulers.

Before the foundation of the SXC and the execution of Operation Falling Star, the United States Air Force suffered from a paucity of purpose-built cargo spacecraft. In desperate need of both tactical and strategic spacecraft, the USAF ordered a number of new ships to be built to support the newly formed SXC. A small handful of these spaceships were already in service near Luna when the rebellion on Mars erupted, but not enough to spare. The Air Force had to come up with an entire wing of heavy, long-haul ships to deal with the Martian situation.

To fill this need, USAF and SXC commanders turned to the civilian market. Dozens of ships were purchased from American corporations for conversion to military use. Most of these were simple bulk freighters or industrial ships: large, heavy, and tough vessels that could stand up to the abuse of a fast, long-distance Mars run. Work on these new ships was prioritized at the small USAF space dock, and engineers and shipwrights contracted through the Weyland Consortium toiled around the clock to prepare the vessels for their journey. Each one was fitted with upgraded engines and control systems. Their interiors were converted to carry troops, materiel, munitions, and aerospace vehicles—everything the First Mars would need to carry out its mission upon arrival.

This desperate Hail Mary plan worked, and the converted ships performed admirably well on the trip to Mars. Indeed, the lessons learned from converting the civilian haulers to SXC ships improved Weyland's and the Air Force's overall knowledge of starship design and construction. Necessity proved once again the mother of invention, and many breakthroughs in aerospace engineering, materials science, and other technical disciplines related to space travel resulted from the crisis.

COMBAT DRONES

SRU-34 "SPECTER" RECONNAISSANCE AND STRIKE DRONE

famous aerospace units operating in the Martian theater. Flying a variety of unarmed shuttles and dropships, the pilots of the Twentieth had a reputation for taking insane risks and navigating under impossible conditions to extract SXC personnel. The Nineteenth Fighter Squadron, also known as the Ground Pounders, was another highly decorated unit piloting heavily armed dropships that flew over one thousand close air support missions. While it served in almost every battle fought by SXC forces, it particularly distinguished itself during the Battle of Kasei Valles. It was during Kasei Valles that the Nineteenth pioneered a particularly daring brand of low-altitude flying that took advantage of the area's rugged terrain—the bravery of its pilots under fire turned the tide of the battle. Although Kasei Valles was considered at best a draw, the exceptional close air support of the Ground Pounders allowed U.S. forces to withdraw their forces, saving countless lives.

COMBAT LOGISTICS FORCE

The Combat Logistics Force (CLF) assigned to the First Mars was composed of technicians and combat engineers and filled a number of roles in the First Mars from construction and maintenance to mining, ordnance disposal, and sabotage. CLF personnel were typically lightly armed, if at all, and operated a variety of heavy equipment used to clear minefields, retrieve damaged fighting vehicles, build structures, and breach fortifications. While the CLF was ostensibly a rear-echelon, non-combat unit, all personnel were trained in combat tactics and the use of weapons. As part of the First Mars, they proved crucial to the Mars mission as they were required for the pivotal role of securing and operating the Bradbury colony's fabrication and manufacturing infrastructure.

During the Siege of Bradbury, specialists of the Combat Logistics Force used their skills effectively and creatively to ensure an SXC victory, the star of which was the Five Hundred Fifty-Fifth Combat Engineering Squadron. Nicknamed the "Triple Nickel," it was led by Commander Wes Maucher, and by the time it laid siege to Bradbury its members had acquired a reputation for efficiency, courage under fire, and a die-hard can-do attitude. During the Siege, Commander Maucher and the Five Hundred Fifty-Fifth were able to secure the megapolis with SXC marine support—effectively trapping the Martians clans in their city. While the Five Hundred Fifty-Fifth and assorted SXC Marine forces made a scene outside of the dome, the Forty-Second Sappers entered Bradbury on a dangerous clandestine mission.

The troopers of the Forty-Second were a combination of commando and combat engineers trained in sabotage and guerrilla tactics. By working with Martian turncoats, the Forty-Second was able to penetrate into Bradbury's Great Dome to secure infrastructure and bring down interior defenses, thereby paving the way for the rest of the First Mars forces. Once inside the main tunnel systems, the Forty-Second delved deep into Clan Cabeiri territory and took control of Bradbury's power generation and life support systems, effectively strong-arming the clans into surrender and ending the siege.

AFTER MARS

Once combat operations ended and the Martian settlements were reorganized under the Martian Colonial Authority, the brigade was recalled to Earth. Although the mission was a success, and the men and women of the First Mars had served with distinction and honor, the brigade did not leave the Red Planet unscathed. Over the course of the long and bloody Martian campaign, the First Mars lost hundreds of good soldiers. While most of these were killed or listed as missing in action, many of its losses were individuals who had deserted during the fighting, taken up with the Martian insurgents, or stayed behind after the recall order was given. Hundreds more were left physically or mentally crippled, held together by medics and comrades until they could return to Earth and Luna for more comprehensive care. The events during the Martian Colony Wars had a lasting, deeply traumatic effect on the men and women of the First Martian Expeditionary Brigade, and fifteen years later the emotional and physical scars are as fresh as the day they were received.

ANDROID

IT IS THE FUTURE.
THE WORLD CHANGED.
PEOPLE DID NOT.

Where does the advancement of technology lead us? Can we learn from our mistakes? Or are we bound to repeat our errors? From cybercrime to the Worlds War, the 272 full-color pages of *The Worlds of Android* present an overview of a future defined by the rise of monolithic megacorps, the creation of true artificial intelligence, labor forces that consist of clones and bioroids, and the colonization of Mars and the Moon.

WWW.FANTASYFLIGHTGAMES.COM